WANTING YOU CLOSE

ARCHER & EVERLEIGH, #2

USA TODAY BESTSELLING AUTHOR
KENNEDY FOX

LAWTON RIDGE DUET SERIES READING ORDER

TYLER & GEMMA DUET

A best friend's brother,
second chance romance

Keeping You Away

Needing You Close

NOAH & KATIE DUET

A best friend's brother,
friends to lovers romance

Pushing You Away

Holding You Close

ARCHER & EVERLEIGH DUET

A brother's best friend,
roommates to lovers romance

Forcing You Away

Wanting You Close

Each duet can standalone, but suggested to
read in order for the best
reading experience.

If you find a girl, hands up, hangin' halfway out on a highway
You find a girl who likes whiskey mixed in her hangover
coffee
Find a girl that scares you half to death
You'd kill to be the train she wrecks
Don't tell her I never met someone like you
Then try and turn her into every girl you ever knew

If you're gonna love her, if you're gonna love her
If you're gonna love, leave her wild

"Leave Her Wild"
-Tyler Rich

CHAPTER ONE

EVERLEIGH

I HEAR something I can't quite place. My eyelids are heavy, and I somehow force them open. When I turn my head slightly, Archer comes into view, and a smile touches my lips. Before I can open my mouth to say his name, my brother stands.

"Everleigh." Tyler walks toward me, and Archer joins him. They look like they haven't slept in days, but relief covers their faces.

"Hey. Where am I?" My voice is almost unrecognizable to me. I try to swallow, but my throat is dry.

"You're in the hospital," Archer states, his voice low. "You got hurt."

I don't remember what happened, but there's a dull ache in my lower abdomen. I'm hooked to an IV with a blood pressure cuff. The constant beeping drives me crazy. "How long have I been here?"

"Two days. You got stabbed, and the doctors did surgery to stop the bleeding," Tyler says.

My eyes widen in surprise because I don't recall any of that. By the expression on Archer's face, there's more to it.

"Wow…" I blink, searching my memory. "Who did it?"

Tyler looks at Archer. "We were hoping you'd know," Archer says.

I shake my head.

The last thing I remember is partying at the bar for Archer's birthday, then going home afterward. Archer and I made love and exchanged I love yous. It was one of the greatest moments of my life. As I meet Archer's intense gaze, I swallow down my emotions because I know I can't say those words to him right now.

Another sharp pain shoots through my body, and I blink hard. I try to reposition myself to get more comfortable.

"How do you feel?" Tyler adjusts my pillow, helping me sit up straighter.

"Like I've been stabbed," I deadpan.

Archer's face hardens, and his jaw clenches, and I realize how upset he is. It doesn't help that we can't talk privately.

"The pain isn't that bad," I try to reassure them, but I assume I'm on some good painkillers.

"The doctors said you'd need to rest for a few weeks," Archer explains. "The wound needs to heal."

I shake my head. "I don't have that kind of time. I have to get back to work as soon as possible. I have new inventory arriving next week."

"It's non-negotiable, Everleigh. You could've died." Tyler glares at me, but his face softens when I narrow my eyes at him. "Don't worry about the shop. Lexie is taking care of it until you can return."

"Thank God," I whisper. I trust her to run things.

This bed feels like it's stuffed with rocks, and I can't get situated with all the wires and tenderness in my stomach. "When can I go home?"

"Could be a couple more days," Archer tells me. "You need to recover from the surgery, and they want to make sure the wound starts healing. It was scary for a bit in the beginning."

I blink at Archer, wishing I could pull him in and kiss his lips.

"We were all so fucking worried about you, Ev," Tyler croaks out. I can tell he's holding back his emotions.

"Do you recall anything from that day?" Archer asks.

"I remember the party…" I say, glancing at him, then at Tyler. He doesn't need to know the details of Archer fucking my brains out the night before.

Tyler speaks up. "So you don't remember anything from that day or who was at the door?"

I shake my head. "No. I'm drawing a blank."

"Damn." He blows out a breath, then glances at Archer.

"I gave the detective the license plates and a brief description of the woman, but I didn't recognize her," Archer admits.

"Better than nothing," I say, wishing he were closer to me. "Are Gemma and Katie here?"

Tyler grins. "Yeah, they literally talked to you for an hour straight after surgery. They were here this morning but left about an hour ago to check on the kids. I'm going to text them and let them know you're awake. They'll be relieved."

I clear my throat. "Is there any way you can get me some water? Maybe let a doctor or nurse know that I'm awake? I have some questions."

"Absolutely." Tyler nods and walks out.

As soon as the door closes, Archer takes my hand and kneels beside the bed.

"Everleigh," he whispers, his voice hoarse with worry as he

3

studies my face. "I've never been so fucking scared in my life. I thought…"

"*Kiss me.*"

Archer doesn't waste any time pressing his soft lips against mine. I fist his shirt, wishing I could pull him onto the bed with me, but our alone time is limited.

"I love you," I say when we pull apart.

"I love you too, baby. The thought of losing you had me ready to burn down the world without an ounce of regret."

I lift a brow. "I kinda like the thought of that. Avenging my death and all."

He shakes his head with a grin. "Making jokes at a time like this is one of your better qualities."

"Will you tell me exactly what happened? I didn't want to ask in front of Tyler."

"It wouldn't have mattered. I already told him everything because I felt like he needed to know the truth." Archer gently sits on the edge of the bed and brushes the hair off my face.

"Everything, *everything*?" I ask with raised brows.

"I didn't tell him about us."

I smirk. "I'm not sure you'd be alive right now otherwise. Okay, well, can you give me a play-by-play on exactly what happened?"

"We were in bed when the doorbell rang. You said you scheduled a breakfast order, so you got up to answer it. I followed you out to go use the bathroom, but then I heard a woman say, 'What do you have that I don't have?' and I knew it wasn't the delivery. When I walked over to ask what was going on, the woman came at you, and I caught you just as you were falling to the floor. I didn't even realize she stabbed you until I saw the blood. She ran and drove off in the same black Escalade that'd been following us. I quickly grabbed my phone and called 911."

"So you saw her face?"

"Yeah, but I didn't recognize her. She had short red hair and dressed like she had money. The look on her face was fucking frightening like she was cracked out and had nothing to lose."

"The only person I know who looks like that is Eric's wife."

"That's what Tyler said too," he tells me. "We gave her name to the police as well."

I squeeze his hand tight. "I'm glad you were there with me. If you wouldn't have been, I might've..." I stop myself from finishing. "I don't want to think about it."

"I don't either." He leans over and brushes his lips across mine again. Just as he pulls away, the door to my room swings open. When I see Lexie's bright smile, my face lights up.

She rushes forward, so Archer steps back to give her space. "Thank God! Do you know how worried I've been?"

I chuckle as she gives me a gentle hug. "I can only imagine. How have things been at work?"

"I'm holding down the fort. Dana and Heidi have been a big help. You don't need to worry."

I let out a relieved breath. "Thank you so much. I really owe you."

She waggles her brows. "I'll send you my wish list."

"Don't make me laugh," I say, holding my stomach.

"Sorry. But seriously, I'm happy to help in any way I can. How are you feeling after surgery?"

"Like I need to track this woman down and return the favor," I remark.

Lexie looks intrigued. "Oh, so you know it was a woman? Any other pieces to the puzzle?"

"Not really. I can't remember shit, which is very frustrating."

Archer randomly makes eye contact with me. Each time I meet his gaze, electricity streams from the pit of my stomach.

"I wonder if it's someone who's been lusting over Archer's pictures and his six-pack." She glances at him, then back at me with a raised brow. "Considering there have been some crazy women coming in and asking way too many personal questions about him. It's gotten around town that you two are *roommates*, so perhaps, this was an act of jealousy." She uses air quotes because she knows more than she should about our situation.

I think about it. "It's actually not out of the realm of possibilities. A lot of women left comments, sent messages, called the store, and even came in and asked about it, so maybe?" Though I'm still leaning toward Natasha, I can't help but wonder. "I wish I could remember. From what Archer said, it sounds like I knew her. So if that's the case, it could've been a customer I'm familiar with."

"Whoever it is, I have an ass to beat for nearly killing my favorite boss ever," Lexie says.

I chuckle, appreciating her protectiveness. Next, she updates me with sales numbers. I inform her about the shipments arriving soon and anything else that comes to mind.

About ten minutes later, Tyler returns with a pitcher of water and a doctor.

"Glad to see you're awake. I'm Dr. Landon." She holds out her hand, and I take it before she continues. "Your brother said you were awake and had some questions." She smiles, showing off her pearly white teeth.

"Yes," I say, sitting up straighter. "A rundown of events would be great."

"Of course. You had lost a lot of blood, so we immediately took you into surgery to stop the bleeding. You were at risk for a hematoma, which means there was blood in places it shouldn't be. Because of the location of the wound and the sutures, you'll be sore and need to rest. That means no work and no heavy lifting. Taking it easy is the key to a full recovery."

I make a face, and she notices. "Your brother already warned me that you don't tend to take breaks, but it's doctor's orders. If you push yourself too hard, you could end up with complications, which would extend your healing time even further," she informs me in a stern motherly tone.

Tyler stands beside her with his arms crossed over his chest and nods in agreement.

"Fine. I'm just not sure how I'm going to survive being down for weeks."

Her eyes soften. "I understand, but it's necessary. You're *very* lucky, Everleigh. Just a few inches to the left and it could've been a lot worse. Luckily, your roommate was home, and you were able to get to the hospital quickly. I've seen people with stab wounds come in too late and not make it out of surgery because of severe blood loss."

The room grows quiet, and I think about the what-ifs. When I meet Archer's gaze, I know he is too.

"Welp, glad that didn't happen." I didn't realize how serious it was. Maybe it's a good thing I can't remember because it sounds like it was painful.

"I think everyone can agree. Once you're released, you'll be on restrictions for at least two weeks. The first ten days are crucial. But it could take months for you to get back to normal."

"*Months*?" My eyes go wide.

7

"Yes. Your body went through something very traumatic, and *strenuous* activities need to be avoided."

She says strenuous as if to imply something else. "Well, that sucks. What about wound care?"

"Your bandage will need to be changed every four to six hours, depending on the drainage. There's a continued risk for infection, so you'll be sent home on an antibiotic."

"And when can I take a shower and go home?"

"You can sponge bath today, but no soaking in water for a while. As far as getting discharged, it could possibly be tomorrow or the next day. I want to make sure you're stable before releasing you. Though the risk is low, there's a possibility of sepsis, and with your blood pressure a little spiked, I'd feel better watching you a bit longer," she explains.

"Okay. Well. That was a lot to take in at once." I chuckle lightly, though I'm not joking.

"I understand completely. You've been through a lot. Do you have any other questions?"

"Not that I can think of right now. Thank you so much. I really appreciate all that you've done," I tell her genuinely.

"You're welcome. If you think of anything else, don't hesitate to call for a nurse. They've got my number, and I'm happy to answer any questions you have. I'll stop in tomorrow."

"Sounds good. Thanks again."

She grins, then leaves.

I swallow hard at everything she said, then remember my dog. "Who has Sassy?"

"Mimi and Pops," Tyler says. "I've kept them up to date with how you've been doing. They've been here every day."

"Wow, I hate that I worried them," I say just as Gemma and Katie rush into the room. They lean over the bed and hug me.

When they pull back, Gemma's wiping her cheeks.

"Don't start that," I tease because I hate seeing her emotional over me.

"We were so upset! It's not easy seeing you like this." Gemma frowns.

"I was ready to track someone down," Katie admits. "Especially after everything we've all been through these past few years. I was worried to death. My PTSD couldn't handle it."

My eyes soften. "I know. I'm sorry that I worried you guys."

"We were ready to *murder* someone," Gemma admits.

Tyler speaks up. "I've already gone to prison once, but I'd do it again."

"Same," Archer adds.

"Add my name to that list too," Gemma says.

"Sorry, but I'm not built for prison life." Katie snorts. "But I'll provide y'all with an alibi to keep you out of jail."

"Oh my God, you guys. Poor Scarlett. She'd have to come live with me."

"Never mind, I take it back." Gemma laughs.

I look around the room, grateful and happy to be alive. I'm lucky to be surrounded by so many people who love me. With all that being said, once I'm better, I'll find out who did this.

After an hour, my body grows tired, and Katie notices. It wasn't that long ago when she was in the hospital after being kidnapped. "We're gonna let you get some rest."

They take their time telling me goodbye before they leave. Then finally, it's just Archer and me.

"You can go if you want," I tell him, not wanting him to feel forced to stay. "You look exhausted."

"I'm not going anywhere, Everleigh."

My heart flutters. "Thank you."

He adjusts my pillow. "You really do need to get some rest, though."

"Will you lie with me?"

A smirk hits his lips. "What do you think the nurse will say when she walks in and sees us?"

"She better mind her own damn business," I say matter-of-factly, patting the space beside me.

Archer hesitates but doesn't make me beg. He gently lies on the mattress and carefully loops his arm around my shoulders. The weight of him feels like home, and I let out a contented sigh. "You're exactly what I've been missing."

He chuckles in my ear, and the warmth of his breath brushes against my neck. "Me too."

CHAPTER TWO

ARCHER

I'VE BEEN at the hospital with Everleigh for the past four days, sleeping in a chair that's as hard as pavement. Then again, I would've slept on the floor if it meant being close to her.

Tyler's been suspicious of my protective behavior since this happened. Regardless, I can't bear to be away from her for too long, especially after almost losing her. Having her blood on my hands as she slipped in and out of consciousness has been a total mind fuck.

The last time I was this worried was the night I got arrested. I'd do anything to protect my sister, and I feel the same about Everleigh. She didn't deserve this, and I hope to God that I'm not the cause of it, but I could be. Lexie's words have been playing on repeat along with what that crazed woman said that night—*what do you have that I don't?*

Yesterday, while Everleigh was resting, I went home and installed motion-activated security cameras around the house. Each corner has one along with a brand-new doorbell cam.

I don't know what else that woman is planning, but I'm not willing to take any more chances.

"You'd think they would've already brought the discharge papers so I can leave." Everleigh groans as she flips through TV channels. She's growing impatient and has been since the doctor said she'd be released today.

"I know," Tyler agrees. "Are you sure you don't need me to take you home?"

"No. My car is more comfortable. Archer can drive it," she tells him with a smirk.

"Okay, okay," he says. When Tyler heard Everleigh would get to leave today, he left work and came up here. He's offered her tons of support while she's been in the hospital and even kept her company while I went home yesterday.

"The next time I'm at a hospital, it better be because Gemma is giving me another niece or nephew," she says matter-of-factly.

Tyler shakes his head. "I'm trying! Trust me! Gotta let my little fellas do their job."

Everleigh pretends to throw up in her mouth. "Please don't talk about your little...nope, no. Just make it happen. *Without* the details, please."

I chuckle, loving their dynamic. While Tyler is a protective hard-ass most of the time, it's also obvious he cares about his sister. After this scare, we've all grown closer.

A food service worker enters the room with a tray of food for Everleigh.

Everleigh looks down at her lunch. "I'm supposed to be leaving."

"You were on my drop-off list, so I'm sure they're still working on getting the sign-offs. As soon as they've got it all taken care of, they'll let you know," he explains before walking out.

Everleigh looks down at the chicken that's white as paper.

Next to it is a green mush that I'm sure is overcooked broccoli and another side of what I assume is mashed potatoes. "And I just lost my appetite. Either of you want this?"

"Nope," I blurt out. "Looks worse than what we were served in prison. I've had enough gross food to last me a lifetime."

Tyler bursts into a roar of laughter. "Holy shit, you're right. There's not enough ketchup in the world that would make that taste good. Is there even any seasoning on it?"

"No," she says, appalled. Everleigh rips the foil off the top of the apple sauce. "At least this can't be messed up. I draw the line at *instant* sweet tea. Like you know it's supposed to be sweet tea, but it tastes like dirty water."

I make a face, and it brings me back to the nasty coffee the prison offered. *Hard pass.*

Moments later, Everleigh pushes away the tray, and a cop enters.

"Please tell me you have my release papers," she tells him, and that's when I notice it's the same guy who took the report the night of the accident.

"No, ma'am. I'm Officer Proctor. I'm glad to see you're awake this time."

"Am I under arrest?" Everleigh teases. "At this rate, it might be the only way for me to break out of this place in a timely manner."

"No." He chuckles. "I'm here to get a statement from you so we can finalize the report on your case. We take this violent act very seriously, and we'd like to find who's responsible for doing this to you. We've gotten some information from your roommate already, but now that you're awake, I wanted to see if you could add anything that might be helpful."

"I only remember the night before I was attacked. It's like my memory was erased."

"Traumatic experiences typically do that," he explains, then pulls out his card. "If anything comes to mind, please call me. We ran the license plate to figure out who it's registered to, but it's under an LLC, so we can't determine who's been driving it. I'll contact you if we find anything else out." He reads out her cell number. "Is that correct?"

"Yep, that's right. Thanks," Everleigh tells him.

"You're welcome. Get to feeling better. We'll be in touch."

Everleigh continues flipping through the channels after the officer leaves. After she's watched two full episodes of *Friends*, she huffs. Before the third one ends, the nurse enters with her discharge paperwork.

"Sorry it took so long. Just needed a few signatures, and it's hard to track people down these days."

The woman goes through all the disclaimers, follow-ups, and privacy acts. After Everleigh has signed her name several times, the nurse offers to get a wheelchair to bring her downstairs.

"Can you help me change?" Everleigh asks her. If Tyler weren't here, I would've been happy to assist.

"Sure." She turns and looks at Tyler and me. We stand, knowing it's time to leave the room.

"I'll pull the car around," I say. Tyler follows as relief washes over me. Having Everleigh back home is something I've been anxiously waiting for. We step into the elevator and make small talk. It's been awkward between us, but it could just be my guilt making something out of nothing. He hasn't asked me if Everleigh and I are a thing, but I wouldn't lie if he did.

"Glad she's going home," he tells me. "Hopefully, she listens and actually takes it easy."

"Me too. Sassy's gonna be happy to see her too."

Tyler grins. "Yeah, she will, though I'm sure Mimi has given her way too many treats. She might've forgotten about everyone else at this point."

I chuckle. "Well, that's what grandmas do."

"Oh yeah. She spoils the hell out of Scarlett, and she's only six months old."

"She's a very generous woman. You're lucky to have her."

He nods. "Don't know what we would've done without her after my mom left. Mimi is an angel."

The doors slide open, and we walk through the halls. Once we're in the parking lot, I scan my eyes around and make sure everything looks okay.

"I'll wait here," Tyler states as I walk toward Everleigh's car.

After I start the engine and move around to the covered area, I tap the brakes a few times just in case that psycho bitch has decided to cut the lines. Though I blame it on my paranoia, nothing is out of the realm of possibilities.

I leave the car idle, then stand next to Tyler as we wait. His eyes move over the area too. "I'm really reluctant to let Everleigh out of my sight," he admits, and I see the worry lines above his brows.

"I am too." I ball my hands into fists, ready to fight anyone —man or woman—who tries to hurt her again.

Tyler frowns. "It's hard because of work and my family. I can't be around her twenty-four seven like I used to, so I'm struggling with it."

"Listen, I promise I'll do whatever I can to keep her safe, and if that means all of my clients get rescheduled until she's fully recovered, then so be it. I can be her full-time bodyguard."

He shakes his head. "I can't let you take on all of the responsibility, Archer. I have a friend I could call to help keep an eye on her, but I'm not sure that's a good idea after what happened to Eric. They still don't know who's responsible for his murder."

"I guess none of us are truly safe, but the truth is you have a family now. Your wife and daughter have to come first. You gotta stay out of danger for their sake. Don't worry, I'll take care of Everleigh like she's my own sister."

Though I mean those words with my whole heart, I hate implying that Everleigh and I aren't anything more than friends. I want to tell him I'm in love with her, but now isn't the time. I'll do whatever it takes to protect her from here on out.

He gives me a tight brotherly hug, knowing what I went through for Annie. "I *trust* you, man. I know you will. Thank you."

"You're welcome." His words cut deep, and I feel as if I've betrayed him by not telling him the whole truth, but I push away the thoughts as soon as I see Everleigh.

I open the car door for her as she's wheeled to the edge of the sidewalk. She meets my eyes, and I help her climb inside the car.

"Stay safe, sis," Tyler says as he hands over her bag, then dips inside and hugs her.

"I will," Everleigh tells him.

I hop in, and we wave goodbye. She winces a bit and readjusts her position. Knowing that this might be an issue, I grabbed a small throw pillow from the couch for her. After she places it against her side, she smiles in relief.

"You good?" I ask before driving away.

She nods. "Better now."

I interlock my fingers with hers on the way. She rubs her thumb across mine. Tonight, I'll get to hold her in my arms as we fall asleep, and that thought comforts the hell out of me.

Tyler follows us, and knowing that he's close also eases my concern. I think it would be impossible for anyone to take us both on, considering we're so accustomed to fighting.

Once we're in Lawton Ridge town limits, Tyler honks a couple of times and waves, then turns off toward the gym. I notice the way Everleigh scans the downtown area, and I search around too, but the SUV isn't in sight. I squeeze her hand as we drive to her grandmother's house. As soon as we park, Mimi comes out with Sassy on a leash.

Her tail immediately wags when she sees Everleigh.

"Calm down," Mimi says, opening the back door.

Sassy jumps in and pushes herself between the seats. "Aw, my sweet girl." Everleigh coos as Sassy licks her face.

"How're you feelin,' honey?" Mimi asks.

"Better. Glad to be going home." Everleigh grins.

"I'm sure you are. Hold on one second," Mimi tells her, then runs inside. When she returns, she's carrying a large bag. "I made some chicken and dumplings for you. I know how much you like those, and it's the perfect weather. Also, I just fed Sassy, so she doesn't need anything until tomorrow."

"I love you. Thank you for takin' care of my baby," Everleigh says.

"I'm so happy you're okay. Take care of her, Archer," Mimi says as she leans in and hugs Everleigh.

"Yes, ma'am. You know I will." I grin, and we say goodbye.

Sassy stays close to Everleigh during the short drive. After we pull into the driveway, I walk around the car and help

Everleigh stand. Sassy jumps out and stays next to her. I wrap an arm around Everleigh and guide her to the door.

"Home sweet home." She sucks in a deep breath and smiles when we walk inside. "I'm so glad to be here."

"Me too. I hate hospitals," I say matter-of-factly.

"Then why did you stay with me?"

"Because I love you and wanted to be close to you."

Everleigh's face softens.

"You hungry?" I ask.

"I'm *starving*. I've eaten garbage for days."

"I'll go grab the food from the car," I tell her, then run outside. Once I'm back in the kitchen, I grab two large bowls and spoons. "Geez, she sent enough to feed a small army." I remove several large containers filled to the brim. "And even then, I could down all of this on my own." Everleigh chuckles.

There's at least a gallon of soup here. I glance up at her. "No way."

"Yeah, I literally become a dumpling afterward." She snickers.

As I fill our bowls, gigantic dumplings splash liquid on the counter.

"I should've warned ya about that," she says. "They can be messy."

"Wanna sit on the couch?" I ask, and she nods.

After I microwave our dishes, I I carry them into the living room, then hand hers over once she's settled with some pillows. Sassy lies on the floor and stares at us with begging eyes.

I taste the first spoonful, and my eyes go wide. "Wow, this is the best soup I've ever had."

"Wait." Everleigh stops eating. "You've never had chicken and dumplings before?"

"Not like this. The ones I've had tasted like chicken noodle soup with slivers or something."

Her jaw nearly falls to the floor. "We've got to introduce you to more Southern delicacies. That's just a travesty. *For real*."

I start laughing. "You're serious about this, aren't you?"

"Abso-fucking-lutely! Mimi's dumplings are the world's greatest," she claims, taking a huge bite out of a fat piece of dough. "Don't tell Belinda I said that, but hers don't touch Mimi's. She gave me the recipe to make my own, but they didn't turn out the same. I swear she uses a secret ingredient."

I chuckle. "I'm so relieved you're home."

She leans into me. "I've missed your warmth."

"I've missed your leg being dead weight on top of mine. And grabbing your ass in the mornings."

"I've missed your cock inside me."

I nearly choke. "About that..."

"Oh, you better not be breaking it off with me. I've been through enough bullshit already," she warns.

"*Never.* But it's another reason you need to take it easy and recover quicker."

"So you can break me all over again?"

I smirk. "You better believe it, sweetheart. No sex until you recover."

She gives me a look of disapproval. "We'll see about that."

After we're finished eating, Everleigh asks if we can watch a movie. Sassy jumps on the couch, and we cover up with a blanket. She snuggles in close to me, and I gently hold her.

"Scary or funny?" she asks, clicking on the Netflix app.

"Lady's choice."

She gives me an evil grin as she starts the first episode of a Ted Bundy documentary. I chuckle at her choice, but then my mind wanders. I think about the woman who stabbed Everleigh, then my thoughts move to Krystal—who I'm still concerned about getting her revenge.

I press my lips to her forehead and she lets out a small sigh of contentment. "This won't ever get old."

"What's that?"

She snuggles a little closer. "Being here with you, just like this."

"I'll never leave you, baby," I say, hoping it's a promise I can keep.

"You better not," she scolds.

I press my lips to hers, running my fingers through her hair, and she moans against my mouth.

"If I wouldn't have gotten shanked, you'd be naked right now," she blurts out when we pull away.

"Be a good girl, and follow the doctor's orders, and we might be able to arrange something soon."

Everleigh gives me an evil grin and slides her hand over my cock. "This is harder than I thought. *Literally.*"

CHAPTER THREE

EVERLEIGH

I⊤ FEELS good to be home and sleeping in Archer's arms again. The last few days since I was released from the hospital have been rough. My body lets me know when I'm exhausted, and I have to slow down. It's been a wake-up call, and I've learned that I can't *go, go, go.* I get fatigued easily, which is annoying, but I'm trying to follow my doctor's orders.

So far, the hardest thing has been not being at work. Thankfully, Lexie keeps me updated with everything going on at the shop, which helps some of my anxiety about not being there. She's loving the extra hours, but I also don't want her to burn out. I owe her a raise and so much more for keeping the boutique running.

As I peel myself off the couch, my phone vibrates. It's a group text from my besties. If it weren't for Netflix, Archer, and my friends keeping me company, I might've already gone crazy. Though, I've been loving the alone time with Archer.

Gemma: So enough time has passed. Spill the fucking beans on what's going on with you two.

Katie: Yeah, we're tired of waiting! At this rate, I'll be a grandma.

Everleigh: OMG. You two are so dramatic!

I laugh and go to my room to grab some clothes before I take a shower.

Archer's in the kitchen, shirtless and eating yogurt.

"Damn, you're just gonna tease me like that?" He scans his eyes down my ripped shirt and baggy yoga pants.

I snort. "Wait. You think *I'm* the tease? No, look at you, *sir.* Might as well be walking around naked showing off your tats like that."

He places a thumb in the band of his boxers, lowering them down to show his hip bone. "I think I can make that happen."

"Ugh," I groan, tempted to do very bad things to him. "Stop it, or you're gonna give me lady blue balls again."

He nearly chokes on his food. "You gotta watch what you say when I'm eating because I don't think you could give me the Heimlich."

"Oh, that's true. I'll make sure you're done swallowing next time."

With a brow popped, he asks, "Going to shower?"

I lean against the doorframe. "You know it. Wanna help? I don't want to slip and fall or anything..."

Archer throws the empty yogurt in the trash, then moves toward me in long strides. My eyes gravitate toward his abs and his sexy V that I want to run my tongue up and down. He notices my mood shift and runs his fingers through my hair when he's close. Before dipping his mouth down, I tilt my head up, giving him the perfect angle to gently slide his lips across mine. I moan against him, wishing I had the strength to please him in all the ways he deserves.

"Let's get you clean, dirty girl," he growls against the shell of my ear, playfully patting my ass.

I swallow hard, then lead us to the shower. Archer carefully undresses me, pulling my shirt above my arms because I still don't have full range of motion. I haven't worn a bra since I was released, so my breasts are on full display.

Archer slides my pants down to my feet, then dips his hands in my panties.

"Baby, you're soaked," he groans, rubbing his finger across my hard nub.

"You do that to me every time."

Archer slowly pulls away and turns on the water, then strips off his clothes.

"Thanks for taking one for the team," I tease with a laugh as he helps me step under the stream. My stomach aches, but I push away the pain.

My primary care physician said I could stop putting on the bandages at my appointment yesterday. The wound is healing as it should, and the sutures will dissolve on their own. I have another follow-up next week and will find out when I'll be released to work.

Archer grabs my body wash and loofah, then cleans down my back and legs.

"This is what being royalty must feel like. I could get used to a strong man washing every inch of my body."

I turn to face him as the warm water streams over my body. His mouth meets mine, and I wrap a hand around his arm to steady myself as he finds his way to my pussy.

"Fuck, baby," he mumbles against my lips, pushing a finger inside and circling my clit with his thumb.

"Oh my God," I hum. I missed this so much.

"You like that, baby?"

I gasp when he adds another. "Make me come," I beg.

He meets my eyes. "Are you sure you can handle it?"

"Don't make me do it myself," I hiss.

He chuckles, thrusting harder. "Yes, ma'am."

It doesn't take long before my body teeters on the edge, and I'm screaming out his name.

"There ya go, baby. Come all over my fingers," he orders.

I lean my body against the wall, knowing I can't hold back any longer. The orgasm crashes so intensely that I nearly lose my balance. Archer holds on to me so that I don't fall but continues to finger-fuck me until I come down from the high. It's incredible how quickly he makes my body unravel.

"Your turn," I say once I catch my breath.

"It's fine, sweetheart," Archer tells me, then licks his fingers off. "You're supposed to be taking it easy. That means minimal labor."

I roll my eyes, then ask, "Okay, then can I watch you?"

He smirks, then grabs himself.

"Show me how you do it," I demand.

Archer puts his hand on the wall above my shoulder, boxing me against his body. He slowly strokes himself as he stares down at me. My pussy squeezes, and I wish I could feel him deep inside me. I love the way he handles his thick cock and how he teases the tip. His movements are mesmerizing as he slowly glides from top to bottom.

"So goddamn hot," I whisper, cupping his balls with one hand and tugging his nipple ring with my teeth.

"Fuck, Everleigh," he groans as he increases his pace.

"Come all over me. Imagine your hard dick being deep inside me, fucking my soft, wet cunt."

"Jesus Christ, Everleigh. I want to," he admits hoarsely as his balls tighten in my grip. "Goddammit, I'd break you in two right now if I could."

"I wish," I say with my full chest. "My body craves you so much. I wanna sit on your face so you can tongue-fuck me."

He groans again as he gives me those bedroom eyes I love so much.

"Shit, I'm close." Archer greedily kisses me as he continues to stroke himself until he grunts and releases over my pussy.

"Mmm." I hum at the warmth of him.

"I love it when you talk dirty." He cups my ass. "My filthy girl."

"Just wait until I'm better. There will be no sleeping for days," I tell him.

"And I won't complain once." Archer grabs the soap and cleans up his mess. After I rinse off, he massages the shampoo into my hair and rubs my scalp. I'm so relaxed after he conditions my hair, I could fall asleep.

"So, this is what being in a healthy relationship is like," I say when we're out of the shower and have dried off.

A cute smile plays on Archer's perfect lips as he wraps a towel around his waist. "I'd say so. Not that I have a ton of experience."

"Me neither, but I know I've never been this happy before," I honestly say.

"I feel the same, baby." He tilts up my chin and presses his lips to mine.

"I think I need some meds," I admit, the pain returning after not taking it so easy in the shower.

"I'll get them for you and meet you in the living room," he offers after I pull my hair up in a towel.

When I walk out, Archer hands me a glass of juice and a

couple of pills. I swallow them down, then sit on the couch and realize I never texted the girls back. Archer takes Sassy outside, and I use that time as an opportunity to reply.

> **Gemma: So you're just going to ghost us instead of sharing? What happened to girl code and sharing all the juicy details?**

> **Katie: You're kicked out of our friend group! It's just Gemma and me now.**

> **Gemma: EVERLEIGH BLACKWOOD! I know you're supposed to be taking it easy, so there better be no hanky-panky happening.**

It hurts to laugh, but I can't help it.

> **Everleigh: Sorry, I was preoccupied. Also, you two are SAVAGES! I get stabbed and need help taking a shower, and you're both ready to divorce me.**

Gemma and Katie send the same cry-laughing emoji.

> **Katie: SPILL IT, WOMAN!**

> **Everleigh: Geez, calm your ass down. After his birthday party, we came home and…**

I give them a dramatic pause, and of course they take the bait.

> **Gemma: and? And? AND?**

Everleigh: We had the most amazing sex of my life and…

Katie: You squirted, didn't you?

My cheeks heat, and I swallow hard, thinking about how he solved my body like a jigsaw puzzle and knew exactly what I needed.

Everleigh: You know way too much about me. But hell, wouldn't you? That man is pure perfection! But that's not all that happened. I told him I'd fallen for him, and he confessed he was in love with me too.

Gemma: Omg! I knew it! I'm so happy for you two. Y'all are literally perfect together.

Katie: Finally! I knew you'd get your happily ever after!

Archer brings in Sassy, then fills her food dish. He speaks to her sweetly, bending down to pet her head as she starts eating.

Everleigh: I've never felt this way about anyone before, and I hate that I have to keep it on the down low, which means NO TELLING TYLER!

Gemma: That's not fair! What if I slip?

Everleigh: Please, Gemma. Please promise you won't.

It would cause more problems, and I'm dealing with enough right now.

Gemma: I can't lie if he asks. That would be wrong.

Everleigh: Listen, I pinky promise to tell him as soon as the time is right. He's a worried mess.

Katie: Don't take too long to tell him, Ev. Gemma's a blabbermouth.

Gemma: Hey! He's my husband. I can't lie!

Katie: HA! Guess that means we need to start planning another wedding?

Gemma: Might as well stop taking your birth control…for Scarlett's sake. She deserves all the cousins!

Katie: LMAO!

Everleigh: Alright, you two have clearly lost it now. BYE.

"What's so funny?" Archer asks as he takes a seat next to me.

I shake my head. "My friends are ridiculous, that's all."

"You're lucky to have them. I wished I had close friendships like that when I was younger. Living here, being with you, and working at a place that doesn't make me miserable…it's like a dream come true."

"That makes me so happy. And I'm glad you're here too. I know things have been rough, but it's gonna get better. I don't want you to worry about me."

"I can't help that. I can't lose you, babe. It would destroy me."

I press a soft kiss to his lips. "I can't lose you either."

The next morning, I roll over and see a dozen roses on the nightstand.

I sit up and find a note.

Happy Valentine's, baby. I love you so much and can't wait to spoil you all weekend.

A smile plays on my lips, and I realize it's the first Valentine's Day when I've been *with* someone. I've never gotten roses from anyone other than my grandparents.

When I enter the kitchen, Archer's piling bacon next to avocado toast and a poached egg.

"Are you serious right now?" I chuckle. "Flowers *and* my favorite breakfast?"

"Oh and this…" he says, then quickly sets our food and

coffee on the table. He rushes to his room, then returns with a box in cupid wrapping paper.

"Now I feel like a jerk," I say because I didn't get him anything.

"Sweetheart, you've been busy resting. Having you sit on my cock when you're better will be the best Valentine's Day gift you could ever give me."

I chuckle. "Consider it an *IOUP* then."

He gives me a pointed look. "I don't know what that means."

"I Owe You Pussy." I shrug, and he snorts. I rip open the paper and pull out black lace lingerie that's more for decoration than support. "This is gorgeous."

He smirks as I hold it up to my body. "And I can't wait to peel it off with my teeth."

"Mmm. It's a date. As soon as the doctor releases me for *strenuous* activities—which better be sooner rather than later." Because I'm ready to sit on his lap right now.

"Don't worry, time will fly," he tells me.

I kiss him and thank him for the gift, flowers, and breakfast. He really is too sweet.

We sit at the table and dig into our food. It tastes amazing, and I nearly inhale it down. Once we're done, Archer cleans up.

"What are your plans today?" he asks while rinsing the dishes.

"Oh ya know, sitting on the couch, scrolling through Netflix, and throwing snacks at Sassy," I say with flat amusement. He turns to give me a look, and I chuckle. "Fine. Besides that, I have some orders to place and want to research the spring trends, so I'll scroll through Instagram and other sites. You could help me pick out some guy's clothing that you like if you wanna help?"

He chuckles. "Sure, sounds like fun."

Since I can't be at the boutique, I do what I can from home. I'm trying to be proactive and stay positive. One good thing that's come out of this has been having time to plan out my launches for the next six months. Though I still get fatigued quickly, I can be on my laptop for a few hours before I have to take a break.

Most of my day is spent on the couch staring at my computer screen, and I have to force myself to get up and walk around. Being in one place for too long isn't helpful and makes me sore. Archer brings me my meds when the pain becomes unbearable and takes Sassy out when she goes to the back door.

Once the sun sets, Archer goes to the kitchen.

"Whatcha makin'?" I peek my head up and meet his eyes.

"It's a surprise," he tells me. "Need anything right now?"

"I'd love to down a bottle of wine, but you know…" I point at my stomach. Since I'm on pain meds, that means no alcohol.

He chuckles. "Not too much longer."

"I hope you're right," I say, then busy myself on my laptop again.

An hour passes and the house smells amazing. Archer has been working hard on whatever he's preparing, and I can't wait to taste it. When I hear him setting the table, I take it as my cue to stand but can't pop up as easily as I'm used to.

Once I'm in the kitchen, my eyes widen at the view. Two plates are filled with spaghetti and meatballs and garlic bread.

"Archer," I gasp. "You've completely outdone yourself."

He pulls out my chair and lowers the overhead lights. "I

31

promised to make it for you one day. Today seemed like the perfect time."

I swallow hard, remembering when he mentioned it all those months ago. We've come so damn far since then. "This is so sweet, thank you."

"Anything for you, baby," he says, sitting across from me.

As soon as I taste the meatballs and garlic tomato sauce, I moan.

Archer lifts his brow. "That's music to my ears."

"This"—I point down at the plate—"is orgasmic."

He grins. "I'm glad. I was scared it wouldn't taste the same, but it does. Brings back a lot of good memories." His gaze meets mine. "And making it for you gives me new ones."

I smile and bite the corner of my lip. "Makes me feel really special."

"You are, babe. You are."

CHAPTER FOUR

ARCHER

AFTER TAKING care of Everleigh for a week, she demanded that I go back to work. I didn't want to leave her side, but she made some valid points that I could no longer argue. She hated being a burden even though I told her several times she wasn't. Since she's not driving or leaving the house yet and five security cameras keep watch outside, I agreed to go back for a few hours a day. Then I made her promise she wouldn't answer the door and to call me if anything happened or if she needed me.

The first morning I go back to work, we eat breakfast together, then I kiss her goodbye.

As soon as I walk to the gym, I go straight to the boxing area. Though I haven't been gone that long, I already feel rusty.

"Good morning!" Tyler sing-songs as he walks up to the ring.

"Morning," I say, checking to make sure everything is ready for my first client.

"How's Everleigh doin'?"

"She's doing great. The doctor said she was happy to see her healing and to keep resting for now. She's just going a little stir-crazy."

He chuckles. "A little? I can't remember the last time she's taken a proper break. I gotta say her work ethic has always been amazing."

"Must run in the family."

He smirks. "She gets it from me."

I chuckle. "But really, she's doing well. I'm taking care of her. Making sure she's eating and not pushing herself too hard."

"Thanks, man. If you ever need someone to keep watch or really help with anything, I have a few close friends on the West Coast who will drop it all to be here."

"I'll remember that. I've kept a close watch on the house, and it seems things have been quiet since the accident. *Really* quiet."

"I don't know if that's a good or bad thing." He lets out a ragged breath. "After the shit that happened to me, then Noah, and now Everleigh, I don't think we can be too careful. It's all kinda fucked me up a bit because I feel like as soon as things start lookin' up, something happens to someone I care about."

"Well, either way, I'll do my best to watch over her when I can."

"Let me put this number in your phone. If you think you need help with anything, and I mean *anything*, call it. I've already let them know."

I hand over my cell, and he adds it in.

"Thanks, Tyler. I'll remember that."

Tyler grins just as Andrew enters with his gloves tossed over his shoulder.

"Damn, I'm glad to see you," he says, patting me on the back.

"Wow, thanks," Tyler deadpans.

I chuckle as Andrew shrugs. Tyler waves goodbye and walks out.

"Ready to get to work?" I ask.

"Hell yeah." Andrew slips on his gloves and steps into the ring. We go over stance and different blocking techniques.

The rest of the hour flies by. Between my lessons, I text Everleigh and check on her.

No news doesn't necessarily mean good news when it comes to stalkers. Whoever tried to hurt Everleigh could be planning their next attack. Add Krystal into the mix of what's already going on, and it's enough to push my worry over the edge.

During my lunch break, I call Annie.

"Archer! Hey, brother." She sounds excited but also tired.

"Can you chat?" I ask since I know she's probably at work.

"I've been on break for about five minutes, so your timing is perfect. How are things? How's Everleigh?"

I fill her in, and she's relieved by the news. She tells me about Sadie and how well she's doing in school. It makes me smile.

"And how are you doing?" I ask.

"I'm doing okay. Staying busy. Keeping Sadie occupied. Just doing the best I can. You know how it is."

"I do." My next client walks in. "I gotta get back to the gym, but I'll talk to you soon. Be safe."

"I will. I love you," she says.

"Love you too. Give Sadie my love."

"You know it. Bye!"

My next three clients are happy to see me, which makes me

glad to be here. The day passes by in a blink, which I'm grateful for. After cleaning the boxing ring and putting everything back in order, I find Tyler and let him know I'm leaving.

"Have a good one."

"You too, man. See ya tomorrow."

I check my surroundings before getting into the car, then send Everleigh a text.

Archer: Want me to pick up something for dinner?

Everleigh: Oooh yesss. I'd like the baked potato soup and triple grilled cheese from the deli. Please!

Archer: You got it, sweetheart. Going there now. Be home soon.

As soon as I walk in, Belinda greets me with a tight hug. She pulls away, keeping her grasp on my shoulders, and looks into my eyes. "How're you doin', sweetie?"

She knows that Everleigh could've died in my arms. In fact, I'm pretty sure the whole town knows at this point.

I suck in a deep breath. "I'm doing alright."

"And Everleigh?"

"She's making awesome progress. Pretty soon, she'll be back to her old self."

"I'm glad to hear it. So I guess you came to get some dinner?"

"Yes, ma'am."

She hands me a menu, but I don't take it.

"Everleigh already gave me her order, and I'm gonna have the same," I say.

"Let me guess…baked potato soup with a fancy grilled cheese."

My mouth falls open. "You're good. So, you wanna tell me what the lottery numbers are for tonight?"

She snorts and shakes her head. "Now, if I could guess that, I might not be standin' here. It'll be right up."

Belinda goes to the back as I wait. When she returns, I hand over my debit card, and she shakes her head. "No, honey. It's my treat."

"Miss Belinda, no…"

"You gotta learn how to accept gifts, son. Now go home and eat before it gets cold."

I laugh and thank her several times before she shoos me away. On the way home, I think about how different my life has been since I moved here. Everyone's always so friendly, and I don't always know how to respond to their generosity.

When I walk inside, Sassy greets me and sniffs the bag of food.

Everleigh pops up with her hair piled on top of her head. "I think I'm glued to the couch."

She reaches for me, and I help her sit up.

"How are you feeling?" I ask, pulling the to-go boxes out, then realize there's more than what we ordered.

"Still sore, but feels like this is becoming my new normal."

"Nah. You'll be healed soon and back to normal.."

"I hope you're right," she says, looking through the food. "You ordered chocolate cake too?"

A chuckle escapes me. "No, Belinda snuck it in. She asked about you, then refused to let me pay."

"Bless her," Everleigh says. "Doesn't surprise me, though. Did you tell her I'm a champ and no one can get me down?"

"Basically," I say, digging into my soup. I look over and notice Everleigh is eating her dessert first.

"Best part of being an adult, I can do whatever I want." She shrugs with a smirk.

"What're your plans tomorrow?" Everleigh asks as we eat.

"I gotta see my parole officer first thing in the morning, then I'm hanging out with this hot chick all day."

"Yeah? Who?"

I meet her eyes. "I dunno. Heard she owns this bougie shop in town. Also, she's super sexy, smart, and gives great blow jobs."

"Ooh, is she single? I've been known to flip flop."

"Is that so?" I ask, intrigued. "Now I'm even more excited."

She grins. "Yep, I'm a man *and* lady eater."

"That's hot, but bitches better back off. I don't share what's mine."

Everleigh bursts into a roar of laughter.

"You have nothing to worry about, babe. You're everything I want and need."

I shoot her a wink. "And I hope to keep it that way."

We continue chatting as we dip our sandwiches into the soup, both agreeing it's the best meal on the planet. Once we've finished, Everleigh gets a call from Lexie, and they talk about the shop.

After I throw away our trash and let Sassy outside, I go to take a shower. Before I can even turn on the water, my phone buzzes with a text from an unknown number.

Unknown: You can keep blocking me, but I'll always find you, Archer. Next time, I'll make sure I kill that fucking mutt too.

I stare at the screen in disbelief that Krystal would put a threat like this in writing. What kind of psychopath could hurt an innocent dog and be proud of it? She's getting braver, which is worrisome. Immediately, I block the number and lock my phone.

After a few deep breaths and trying to gain control of my anger, I step into the shower and hope the hot water washes away my rage. I'm not an inherently violent person, but when it comes to Everleigh, I'll do whatever it takes to keep her safe. Sassy too.

By the time I'm clean, I'm calmer but still feel uneasy. I go to my bedroom and find Everleigh tucked under the covers. She tilts her head and looks at me.

"Somethin' wrong?"

"Nah. Just have some things on my mind."

She smiles. "Come snuggle with me."

"Don't have to tell me twice."

Once I'm under the sheets, Everleigh scoots closer until her ass presses against me. I hold her to my chest.

The next morning, I kiss Everleigh goodbye before I leave

to meet my parole officer. I've seen him a few times already, but this time I'm more anxious than usual.

When I enter, Calvin is sitting behind his desk. I have to piss in a cup to make sure I'm not breaking any of my probation rules. I happily do it because I'm clean and always have been. It's protocol, but I understand why it's in place.

Once I'm done, I sit across from him.

"So, fill me in with what's going on."

I suck in a deep breath, not sure where to start, but knowing I have to tell him the truth. "There's been a lot."

"Go ahead," he encourages.

"My girlfriend was stabbed and had to have emergency surgery."

The man deserves an Emmy because he doesn't react. "Is she okay?"

"Yes, she is. She'll fully recover, just taking it easy now."

"That's good news. Do you know who did it?"

"I don't. That's why I'm worried. Not to mention I've been receiving threatening text messages from Krystal, Chad's sister."

"Archer, you need to file a report. They can't charge her without proper evidence, so it needs to be documented now. That way, if her threats become actions, a file has already been started."

I listen to his every word, remembering how I stressed the same things to Annie when she was with Chad. The realization that the situations are familiar nearly knocks the breath out of me.

"You're right. I'll go to the station after I leave here."

"Archer, if you need me for anything, please don't hesitate to reach out. I just don't want you to get caught up in something that's not your fault. Understand what I mean?"

I nod. "Absolutely."

"Anything else you want to discuss?"

"That's about it. I love being in Alabama. It was the change of pace I needed."

"I'm happy to hear that." He looks down at his calendar. "We should meet in sixty days unless a reason pops up that we need to meet sooner. Go to the police after you leave here and show them the text messages. Then send me an update."

"I will. Thank you," I tell him, standing. I shake his hand, then leave.

When I'm in the car, I scroll through all the messages I've gotten over the past month. I slam my fist against the steering wheel, the realization setting in that Krystal isn't going to leave me alone—but I'm not going to let her get away with it any longer.

CHAPTER FIVE

EVERLEIGH

For the past couple of weeks, I've had a lot of ups and downs. I don't like lounging around for too long and am often bored.

Though I enjoyed having Archer take care of me and being around, I felt bad I was keeping him from work. Between him and Tyler constantly worrying about me, I was more than ready to get back to work.

I can't lift anything over fifteen pounds for another month per doctor's orders. I've been doing physical therapy exercises at home to prepare me for my first shift back at work today.

"Ev, you look so good," Lexie says when she walks through the front door. "You're here early."

"I couldn't get out of my house fast enough," I tell her as she gives me a gentle hug. "I can only watch Netflix for so long before I go stir-crazy."

"I figured you would've loved being locked in with Mr. Hunky Roommate," she taunts, grabbing the clipboard and looking at today's task list.

"Oh I did, but it's more of a tease than anything since he'd walk around shirtless and wouldn't let me touch him below the waist. He took his job of making sure I rested a bit *too* seriously, if you know what I mean."

"Aw…I bet he was happy to take care of you, though. Archer seems like good company."

"Yeah, he was. I just hate being fussed over, ya know?"

"That's because you're independent to a fault." She shrugs, then heads to the back. "I'll get these racks unloaded."

"Don't baby me." I scowl. "I can hang stuff!"

Lexie chuckles, rolling the rack of clothes to the front of the store. "Yes, boss, I know."

Heidi comes in a few hours later, and I take my lunch break, though I'm not super hungry. My appetite hasn't quite returned since the accident.

Archer: How's your first day back?

I read Archer's text as soon as I sit at my small desk.

Everleigh: Lexie's treating me like a baby, so don't worry about me doing too much.

Archer: Good, then she's earning her raise.

Everleigh: Did you tell her to keep an eye on me?

Archer: I told everyone who would listen to make sure you're not overdoing it.

I roll my eyes and sigh, though I appreciate where his heart is.

Everleigh: Babe, I love you, but you're worrying too

much. The doc cleared me. My wound is basically healed. I'm fine. I mean, I'd be better if my boyfriend would finally rail me...

Archer: Don't think I haven't wanted to, but I don't want to hurt you.

Everleigh: PLEASE...HURT ME!

I add a few eggplant and water drop emojis, to which he responds with an eye roll and tongue-sticking out emoji.

Once my break ends, I continue checking out customers because it's the least taxing. Everyone has heard about the incident, so I've been asked about it at least a dozen times. By the end of my shift, I'm more mentally exhausted than physically.

"Alright, I'm out before I hear 'oh honey' one more time after I explain where I've been," I tell Heidi, who chuckles and gives me a side hug.

"Oh honey, you poor thing. I just hate that someone's out there stabbin' people for no good reason," she mocks in a thick Southern accent.

I burst out laughing, grateful it no longer hurts to do so. "Yep, you nailed it."

As I drive home, I spot a very sexy man on the sidewalk and slow down.

"Hey good lookin', you want a ride?" I shout out the window. "Or perhaps I can ride you."

"Well aren't you full of Southern charm," he drawls. "Let me see that sweet rack first."

Archer waggles his brows as he walks over to the car.

"Don't you tease me. I'll strip right here," I tell him.

"I know you're bluffing, but damn that'd be a sight to see." He gets inside the car, and I drive us home.

After we pull into the driveway and walk inside, Archer takes a shower. I dig around in the fridge to see what I can make. Though I wasn't hungry at lunch, I'm starving now and am craving pasta.

"Whatcha making?" Archer enters with a towel wrapped around his waist. My eyes linger on his nipple piercing and tattoos because staring at him never gets old.

"I think I want chicken fettuccini Alfredo, but now I'm reconsidering starting with you." My gaze drops to his cock.

Archer slowly steps backward when I try to get closer. "I better get dressed and stop the temptation then."

"Ugh, damn. You're such a tease!" I pout, trying to yank the towel off him, but he secures it to his waist. "C'mon, four weeks is long enough!"

"We waited over two months the first time. I think you can wait a few more days."

My face drops. "I'm about to go get BUB and let him do the job for you."

Archer chuckles, making his way down the hallway. "As long as I can watch."

I've been back at the shop for five days, and I finally feel like life is returning to normal. Archer's still taunting me with his six-pack abs and kissable lips, but thinks I'm too fragile to be thrown around a bed. By the end of the weekend, my goal is to prove him wrong.

Today, the girls and I are going shopping in Mobile for bridesmaid dresses. Though Katie's wedding is in a few months, my whole *needing to recover* has set us back by a few weeks.

"Are you seriously walkin' around with that thing?" Katie asks, eyeing my self-defense keychain.

"Damn right. Ready to tase, pepper spray, or poke a bitch if they come within five feet."

Gemma snorts as we walk toward the store. "What's on it?"

"Well…" I hold it up for her to see. "Tyler got it for me, and at first, I was reluctant, but then I figured why not. Now it's a habit to carry it. The key knife is pretty badass, and the alarm is really loud. Plus, it gives Archer peace of mind."

"Don't show that to Noah. He'll make me get one just for the sake of it," Katie says as I open the door.

Before I can respond, we're greeted by a saleswoman eager to make her commission. Since this is a no kids day, we drink champagne as we shop for dresses and shoes. It's given me the opportunity to reconnect with my best friends away from Lawton Ridge.

"That's my favorite one on you," Katie says as I stand in a baby blue dress. "Really matches your eyes."

"I agree." Gemma smiles wide as I adjust the bust.

"Too bad my tits don't fill it in," I mumble.

"I doubt Archer's complainin'." Katie smirks. "The way that man looks at you puts Hallmark to shame."

"I remember that early honeymoon phase. It's seriously the best." Gemma sighs, then takes a long sip of her drink.

"As if you two aren't still in it," I tease, looking in the mirror and imagining Archer ripping it off me after the reception.

After three hours of drinking and trying on gowns, Gemma and I make a decision. Since we're both the matron and maid of honors, Katie let us choose between three colors and the style we wanted. I fell in love with a backless midi dress that accentuates my ass. If Archer doesn't rip it off me with his teeth, I'll scream out in protest.

"Alright, I need to eat. Where do you wanna go?" Katie asks as she pulls out of the parking lot.

"Someplace that'll soak up this champagne," Gemma states.

"Carbs it is!" Katie chuckles, though she stopped drinking hours ago.

We go to a small Italian restaurant and order pasta with unlimited breadsticks.

"So do the police have any leads?" Gemma asks once the server brings us our drinks and food. "Tyler mentioned he hasn't heard anything."

I shake my head. "There's not enough info. Archer's description is vague, and I can't remember shit," I explain, irritated that my memory hasn't come back yet.

"Well, if it's not Natasha, could it be someone obsessed with Archer?" Katie asks, biting into a breadstick.

"Lexie mentioned that when I was in the hospital. It's the only theory that makes any sort of sense." I shrug. "But I'm not convinced it *wasn't* Natasha. After the way she bitch slapped me at your baby shower, I have a feeling she lost her mind after Eric died."

47

"Still shocking that none of us knew he was married," Gemma says, twirling a forkful of pasta. "I told Tyler he should go pay her a visit."

"You encouraged that?" I ask.

Gemma shrugs. "Tyler's scary when he's on a mission. Nearly unstoppable."

"Until you find his tickle spots," I say, laughing and nearly choking on my sweet tea.

"I'm tellin' him you said that." Gemma smirks.

"Imagine if all three of our men showed up at her doorstep. That might send a clear message," Katie adds.

"While they're in Vegas, might as well ask Liam and Mason to join in on the fun," I suggest.

"I never met them. But I've heard good things," Katie says.

Tyler became friends with Liam Evans and Mason Holt when he lived in California years ago. He trained them to box, but then some shit went down, and Tyler got involved. They've been there for each other through thick and thin. If Tyler asked for a favor, they'd both jump.

"You think Lawton Ridge is full of drama? Tyler told me all kinds of stories from when he lived there," I say. "But hey, him landing in prison is what brought him back here."

Gemma snorts. "Silver lining, I guess."

Chuckling, I nod. "I can't believe Tyler, Noah, and Archer have all been in prison at some point."

Katie and Gemma's expressions go flat.

"What does that say about us?" Katie asks, and we burst out laughing.

A table of four older women stares at us in shock. I swear they're about to have a stroke by the way their expressions are stuck.

"Don't worry, just because incest is illegal doesn't mean it should be," I tell them in complete seriousness. "It's like the government has something against true love, amiright?" I ask loudly in a thick Southern drawl.

Their eyes nearly pop out of their heads as they blink at me wearing scowls.

"Oh my God, Ev," Gemma mutters, trying to suppress her laughter.

"I'm pretty sure that was the standard in biblical times." I shrug.

"In royal families too," Katie adds.

"Right!" I agree.

Seconds later, the four women flag down their server and ask for their checks.

"Guess they can't take a joke?" I shrug when they leave.

"They should be happy you didn't bring up penis sizes again," Katie says.

"I mean, what else are we supposed to talk about on girls' day out?" I flash a cheeky grin. "Though, now that Gemma married my brother, it'd just be weird to have that convo."

"And Katie's marrying *my* brother, so yeah, let's not go there," Gemma adds.

"Well, Archer isn't related to either of you, so he's fair game." I waggle my brows. "Though, I'm sure y'all can guess just how *happy* he makes me."

"Unlike Scotty Preston in eleventh grade." Katie snorts. Scotty was a one-time hookup for one *small* reason only.

"Look, I know it's not all about the size of the prize, and teeny weenies need love too. Just not from me." I shrug.

The server decides to come over and ask if we need anything else at that moment.

We finish our lunch and are laughing as we walk to the car.

We stop when we see Katie's tires have been slashed and the word SLUT is written on the back window.

"*Oh my God…*" Katie gasps.

"Wow…those ladies really didn't like us," Gemma says, and I nudge her.

"I don't think it was them, Gem."

I wrap my arm around Katie. "I'm so sorry. I'll pay for this."

She furrows her brows. "Why? This isn't your fault."

I give her a look that says otherwise. Immediately, I scan the area and hold out my keychain of weapons. Whoever it is, they followed us here and could still be lurking.

Katie calls roadside assistance and explains the situation. It takes two hours before we're finally on the road and heading home. While we waited, I called Archer to let him know what happened, and he's ready to glue himself to my side. I hate that this brings him more worry, but I refuse to let this person control my life.

"This is ridiculous. Whoever's doing this is a fucking coward." Katie's still seething when she pulls into my driveway, but I don't blame her. I hate that whoever's after me is now including my friends.

"Babe." Archer pulls me into his arms as soon as I open the door. "You okay?"

"I'm fine, just pissed." I sink into his warmth and kiss his lips.

Sassy rushes to my feet, and I lean down to pet her. "Were you a good girl today?"

"She's been a lazy shit, then stole my sandwich right off my plate when I wasn't looking."

I crack up, then shake my head. "No treats for you, I guess."

Later that night, when we're lying in bed, I turn to him. "So there's something we need to discuss."

"Alright…" he says cautiously.

"Since Gemma and Katie know we're together, I think it's time to tell Tyler. That way we can finally be together in public without worrying that it'll get back to him."

"If you think it's time, then I'll do it." He holds me tighter. "Just know that he might punch my face in."

I snort, wrapping my leg over his body. "And if he does, I promise to make it all better."

"Everleigh…" he warns when I rub over his cock that's hard and ready.

"You seriously gonna make me go solo another night?" I ask.

"It's a much safer option."

I release a loud groan, then crawl over him and off the bed. "Fine. I'll be in my bed with BUB."

Determined to follow through with my threat, I march toward my room, then grab BUB from my nightstand. As I lie down and spread my legs, I place the vibrator over my clit. If Archer's going to withhold orgasms, then I'll do it myself.

"Slide your panties to the side," Archer's demanding voice captures my attention as he leans against the doorframe.

Instead of telling him he lost his chance, I comply. He licks his lips as he watches me, and my breathing picks up as I race to the edge.

"You're so wet, baby," he says in a hoarse voice.

I squeeze my breast with my free hand, then let my knees fall to the sides. I'm spread wide open for his viewing pleasure.

"*Fuck.*"

I press the button to speed up the vibrator. My back arches

as I climb closer to release, and I love that Archer's watching my every move. The heat in his gaze pushes me further, and I know it won't be much longer.

"I'm so close," I whimper.

Just before my body can fully reach climax, the vibrator is ripped from my hand, and Archer's towering over me.

"Hey!" I squeal. "That was cruel."

"You don't come without me," he orders, tearing my panties off me.

"You weren't willing to do the job so I resorted to other options."

He groans in my ear. "Keep your hands on the bedrails. I'm gonna prove that I'm your *only* option."

I can hardly control my breathing to respond, then he moves between my thighs and takes over. The warmth of his tongue hits me hard as he slides up my slit and captures my greedy nub between his lips.

"Oh my God. *Please, Archer*. I'm desperate," I beg, lifting my hips to meet his face.

"What do you need, sweetheart?" he taunts, softly biting the inside of my leg.

"You. Right. *Now*." I'm tempted to shove his face back to my pussy if he doesn't give me what I need.

"You gonna squirt all over me, baby?"

"If you hurry the fuck up," I grit out, and the vibrations of his laughter tickle my thigh.

Without responding, Archer sinks two fingers deep inside me, and I yelp in surprise. His mouth covers my clit as he thrusts hard.

"*Yesyesyes*, sooooo close." My hips buck, and Archer holds me down with his free hand.

He continues his sweet assault as tingles shoot down my

spine and explode between my thighs. Archer continues to finger-fuck me as I moan and scream his name. The feeling is so damn intense, I can't control how my body shakes against him.

"There's my good girl. Squirt all over me." Archer licks his lips as he watches me and pulls his fingers out. As soon as I relax, he returns and works me up to another release.

When my body is spent, Archer lifts me and hauls me over his shoulder.

"What are you doin'?" I squeal, clinging tightly to his back.

"Gettin' you in the shower where I can fuck you raw." He smacks my bare ass, then sets me down on the bathroom counter.

"Oh my God, that's cold." I squirm as I adjust to the temperature change.

Archer smirks as he turns on the hot water, then strips off his pants.

"I hope you weren't lying about being ready for this because, baby, I've been dreaming about being inside you for weeks."

I chew on my bottom lip and grin. "If you don't break me in half and have me screaming in a foreign language, I'll be disappointed."

Archer drags me to my feet and into his bare chest. He tilts up my chin and presses his lips to mine. "You're so goddamn dirty, you know that? I'm about to fuck the English out of you."

CHAPTER SIX

ARCHER

After Everleigh was in the hospital, I've been more protective than ever before. Keeping her at a distance while she healed was a struggle, but after she insisted she was ready, I caved. And I can't say I'm sorry about making love to her.

Everleigh lights something inside me that I can't explain, and though we're still trying to figure out who's after us, I've never been happier. Holding her in my arms each night and hearing her scream my name as she comes all over me is fucking heaven. But now the time has come to let Tyler know. It's been a couple of weeks since Everleigh and I discussed it, and the longer I wait, the more I feel like shit for betraying my best friend. Regardless of the consequences, I need to face them before he finds out from someone else.

I haven't decided *how* to tell him yet, but hopefully, I can get some time with him after work today. I'm scheduled with back-to-back clients and barely get five minutes to use the bathroom or eat. But regardless, I've decided I'm doing it.

"Hey, man. Your two o'clock just canceled. Wasn't feeling

well," Tyler tells me as he grabs a pair of gloves. "So, figured I could come box with you for a bit and catch up."

I raise my brows as he enters the ring, stretching out his arms like he's ready to kick my ass.

"That okay?"

I shrug, hoping he can't see my fear. Tyler has years of experience on me and could easily hurt me if he wanted. "Sure. I'll go easy on ya," I taunt.

Tyler chuckles. "Well, how are things goin'? Everleigh says she's feeling better, but is she really?" He circles me, taking a swing, but I dodge it.

I think back to the past two weeks. I've either bent her over and ate her pussy, fucked her against the wall, or had her squirting all over me as I pounded into her.

Great, now I'm getting hard imagining it.

Tyler gets a hit in as I replay all the dirty scenes.

I shake it off and try to focus. "Yeah, she's been fine. Seems like she's gotten her energy and spunk back." Circling around him, I throw a right hook and connect with his jaw.

"Good. Sometimes, she'll just tell me what I wanna hear so I'll stop askin'," he explains, and I smile because that's just how she is.

Tyler goes in for an undercut and gets me right in the gut. Before I can recover, his fist jabs my face.

Stumbling to my feet, I return to my stance and keep my eyes on him. Tyler's quick and calm, never giving away his next move.

"So how about you? How are you doin' since all this shit started?" he asks when I swing and graze his cheek. He's too quick on his feet.

"Alright, I guess. I'm finding my place here, so no

complaints. Though there is something I've been meaning to talk to you about."

It's now or never. If Tyler wants to kick my ass, at least I'll have gloves to block some of his hits. But I can't keep lying to him, not when he's the reason I'm even here.

"Okay, what's up?"

We continue circling each other, and I eventually just spit it out.

"I'm in love with your sister."

Without a second thought, Tyler throws a right hook into my nose. There's a flash of anger in his eyes.

"I'm sorry, man. I tried to stay away," I say, dodging another swing, but then he lurches his other arm right into my stomach. It's so forceful, he nearly knocks the wind out of me.

"Does she feel the same?" he asks.

"Yes, it's mutual," I admit, hitting him just as hard.

Tyler throws punches until I land on the floor. I hold up my arms to block him until he tires out, but I underestimated his stamina. He's on top of me, swinging with a vengeance, and though he has every right to be pissed, I won't take this lying down.

I drive my knee up and curl my body to the side, taking him with me. As soon as he's down, I jump to my feet. Tyler quickly stands, not giving me much time to catch my breath.

"*If you hurt her…*" he begins, his expression serious. "I won't be using gloves next time."

Before I can respond, he kicks out his leg, and I fall.

"Argh," I groan as soon as my back slams onto the floor. He's not fighting fair, and he knows it.

Tyler stands over me with a cocky smirk, amusement written all over his face.

"What?" I croak out, waiting for his next illegal move. I wouldn't be surprised if he kneed me in the nuts.

He shakes his head. "I already knew, you dumbass."

Tyler holds out his hand, nodding for me to take it. When I do, he helps me to my feet. As I fight to catch my breath, Tyler's expression changes from angry to humored.

"What do you mean you knew?" I pull off my gloves.

He snorts. "You two are so fucking obvious, c'mon. I'm not *that* dense. The way you look at each other and how protective you are of her—which is one reason I didn't confront you sooner—and how happy she's been. I've known for a while but was just waitin' for you to man up and tell me yourself."

I blink in shock because I thought we were careful, but I guess not. Tyler knows us both so well, I should've known he'd figure it out.

"So, you're not mad?"

"Well, not as much as I should be," he confirms. "I'm pissed neither of you listened to my warnings, but ultimately you're grown and can make your own choices. Just know they come with consequences if you break her heart."

"Alright, fair enough." I grin, relief washing over me.

Tyler slaps me on the back. "I knew it was only a matter of time before you won her over."

"More like, she won *me* over…I tried just being friends, but our feelings and attraction became too strong to ignore."

"Yeah, I don't need the details, okay? The less I know, the better. As long as y'all are happy, then I'm cool."

I laugh, patting his shoulder. "Got it, thanks."

After my shift ends, I walk home and am greeted by Everleigh. Before I say a word, I go to her in the kitchen and cup her face, crashing my lips to hers.

"Now that's the hello I expect when you come home every day," she says when we finally come up for air.

"I missed you." I press a kiss to her nose. "I told Tyler today."

Her eyes widen. "You did? Oh my God, is that why you look like you got your ass beat?"

"Hey, I *let* him hit me," I tell her as I grab a drink from the fridge.

She snort-laughs. "How'd he take it? Should I be expecting him to barge in at any moment?"

"After punching me in the face and kicking my legs out from under me, he admitted he already knew. Threatened if I broke your heart, he'd make sure I was in real pain. Then said he was happy for us."

Everleigh laughs, wrapping her arms around my neck. "I'm relieved it's out there. Now we can go on our deli date and be together in public. Oh, and go to Jerry and Belinda's reception as a couple."

"Mmm…sounds like a good time." I spin around and hold her to my chest. "Guess I better cancel my plus-one for that."

She pulls back slightly, furrowing her brows. "Excuse me? What?"

"Well, we never said we were exclusive. Figured it'd keep people off our track if I brought someone else to the party."

My tone is serious though I'm about to burst at the evil eye she flashes me. Seconds later, I crack into a full-on laugh.

"Do you have a death wish, Archer Boone?" She pushes me, but I quickly grab her wrist and pull her back to me.

"Sometimes, you're just too easy to mess with."

"Do it again, and I'll give Tyler permission to really beat your ass." She pokes me hard in the stomach. "And for your information, we are definitely exclusive. I don't care what you say."

Chuckling, I shake my head in amusement. "Baby, I've been exclusively yours since the moment we met. I don't tell just anyone that I love them." I tuck loose strands of her hair behind her ear and bring my mouth closer. "If anyone tried touching you the way I do, I wouldn't think twice about going back to prison for ending them. Just remember that the next time you try to make me jealous."

"Oh come on, that was one time." She groans.

"And that was enough." I flash her a wink, then lower my palm to swat her ass. "What should we make for dinner?"

After receiving another suspicious text this morning, I've been contemplating telling Everleigh about them. The last thing I want to do is worry her more than she already is. It's been stressful, but I don't want to keep hiding it either. I'd rather she know in case she gets them too.

After cooking us chili and cornbread, I decide to bring it up as we sit on the couch. "I've been getting some messages from an unknown number, and some of them are weird." My words immediately grab her attention.

"Like what?"

"One was about Sassy, and whoever it was implied they had been in the house," I explain.

"Oh my God, Archer. How could you not tell me this?"

"I didn't want to freak you out," I say calmly, resting my palm on her knee. "We have cameras up now, so I assumed whoever did it wouldn't be stupid enough to try again."

"I knew someone was in here and gave something to Sassy!" She grinds her teeth together.

"Krystal's just trying to get under my skin, so I don't bother responding. I've blocked every number."

"Who's Krystal?"

"Chad's sister."

"Oh. I don't think you've ever said her name before. You really think it's her?"

"Yeah, she called me once, and I recognized her voice. She talked about how I took away the only important person in her life and mentioned Chad."

She stops eating. "When did that happen?"

"After our trip to see Annie and Sadie."

"That was two months ago!" As she stands, my hand drops, and I know she's furious. "Why did you keep that from me?"

"Baby." I get to my feet and meet her eyes. "I didn't want my past to ruin what we had and worry you."

"You didn't think that was crucial information for me to know? What if she's the one who stabbed me?"

"I saw the woman's face. It wasn't her."

"How can you be positive? It's been years since you've seen her. She could've changed or had plastic surgery for all you know. Women dye their hair all the time."

"I don't think so, but..." I shrug.

"Wait, you said her name was Krystal, right?"

"Yeah." I follow her to the kitchen, where she grabs a bottle of water. "I had an out-of-town customer come into the boutique like a month before the incident. She said her name was Krystal, but her friends called her Kay."

My heart races as I think about Krystal being in Lawton Ridge. If she was brave enough to go into Everleigh's shop, who knows what else she's capable of.

"What'd she look like?"

"I don't entirely remember. I wanna say she had short jet-black hair, and she talked with a weird accent. That's how I knew she wasn't a local. She asked about you a lot, but I didn't think much of it because it was an everyday occurrence after your pictures went live. In fact, Lexie and I were talking about it right before she walked in." Everleigh leans against the counter, and I can tell she's deep in thought. "A week before that was when I noticed Sassy was acting weird, and things were moved."

"It could've just been a coincidence," I offer, though I don't think anything about our situation is coincidental.

"I wish you would've told me sooner," she says with a deep sigh.

I step closer, grabbing her hands and placing a kiss on her knuckles. "You're right. I'm sorry. No more secrets."

"Between Natasha and Krystal, we have to tell each other everything. Even if you think it's going to stress me out."

I cup her cheek and nod. "Promise, I will."

"So let's assume it was her. Do you think she was watching us?" Everleigh asks when we return to the couch.

"Most likely watching me, yes. Might've followed me home, saw you, followed you to work, and tried to get more details out of you. Then later, broke into the house to snoop around before confronting you."

"What would she be looking for?" Everleigh asks.

"Honestly, no clue. Best guess is she's just trying to find something to threaten me with, which is you and Annie. She's always been mentally unstable, but I have a feeling it got worse after Chad died."

"Great, another crazy woman who wants me dead."

"Well, I told my parole officer, and he suggested that I report it to the local police. There's not much they can do, but at least it'll be documented if she does something."

She nods, petting Sassy as she processes everything. I hate that I had to share the great news about Tyler approving of us with this fucked-up news about Krystal.

"Try not to worry, okay? Our home is secure, and when we're not at work, we'll stick together or with friends. Got it?"

"Damn, there goes my solo middle-of-the-night strolls," she deadpans.

"You little smart-ass." I grab her face and press my lips to hers. "I'm going to do whatever it takes to protect you, got it? If Krystal wants to hurt you, she'll have to go through me."

"I hate that I can't even open my front door anymore without fear," she murmurs. "And I hate even more that I can't remember who attacked me."

Though we've speculated it was Natasha, there's zero proof. The detective had someone draw a sketch based on my description, but they haven't been able to track her down to question her whereabouts.

"I know, baby."

Once we've finished eating, I take Sassy out, then clean up the kitchen. Everleigh calls for me, and I follow her voice to the bathtub.

"We haven't soaked together yet. Wanna join me?" She moves slightly so the tops of her breast peek over the soap suds.

"Hell yes." I waggle my brows, then remove my clothes. Everleigh watches closely, keeping her gaze on the happy trail that leads to my cock.

"Have you ever heard the phrase *it's not nice to stare*?" I tease, sliding in behind her and pulling her back to rest against my chest.

"I'm only admiring what's mine," she retorts as her head drops to my shoulder.

"Mmm…is that so?" I whisper in her ear, slowly sliding my hand down between her thighs.

"I can't help it. I'm a *very* lucky woman."

"You have no idea what that means to me, baby." I suck on her neck and rub circles over her clit. "I don't feel worthy of you."

She turns her head and captures my mouth. "I've never told another man I love them, but I knew without a doubt I was in love with you. I hope you realize you're more than worthy of me."

A grin spreads across my face. Everleigh has a way of doing that to me. Even when I don't feel like smiling, she pulls it out of me.

"And I'll gladly spend the rest of my life proving it to you even if I don't believe it." I flash her a wink, then thrust a finger inside her.

"Oh my God," she yelps in surprise. "Yes, more of that…"

As my hardness presses against her back, I finger-fuck her pussy and massage her breast. She twists her arm between us and grabs my shaft, stroking me as hard and fast as she can.

I continue until she's squeezing and squirting all over my

fingers. As I pinch her nipple, she moans out my name, and I nearly explode at her tight grip around me.

"Sweetheart, turn around and ride me," I demand. Thank God for her massive tub.

Everleigh stands and moves over me before sliding her body down on my dick. She immediately starts rocking, and her tits in my face are too sexy to resist. I pull one into my mouth, then slide my tongue around her nipple before moving to the other. I lift my hips and thrust deeper inside her as she holds my shoulders.

"Fuck, you look beautiful bouncing on my cock." My hoarse voice gives me away—I'm so damn close to exploding.

I lower my hand between us and find her greedy clit so she can come with me.

"Archer, yes, right there," she moans, rolling her head back.

My balls tighten as her cunt squeezes my dick, and I know we're teetering on the edge together. I lower my free hand to her ass, cupping and squeezing it. Everleigh bites her bottom lip, and when her mouth opens with a groan, I slide a finger between her ass cheeks until I find her tight hole.

"Holy shit," she squeals as I add pressure.

"That feel good, baby?" I ask in her ear.

"Don't stop," she begs.

I tease her ass as she rides me faster, and as soon as her back arches, I know she's squirting down my cock.

"That's my good girl," I praise moments before I release inside her.

She collapses against me and mutters, "Wow…that was *intense*."

I chuckle when she releases a sweet-sounding contented sigh. "Let's go clean up in the shower."

"Okay, but you may have to carry me. I think I lost feeling in my legs."

I laugh while standing and pulling her up with me. Once I dry my feet on the towel, I pick her up and launch her over my shoulder.

"Not like this! I meant in a romantic way," she scolds.

Chuckling, I smack her ass and walk toward the other bathroom. "This is as romantic as I get."

CHAPTER SEVEN

EVERLEIGH

"How do I look?" Archer comes from around the corner wearing slacks and a button-up shirt. The sleeves are rolled to his elbows, which I find sexy as hell. I move toward him as my heels click on the floor, then I press a soft kiss on his lips.

"Like you want me to ride your face for the rest of the afternoon," I say seriously when I pull away.

He checks his watch. "Well, if we didn't have to be there in fifteen minutes, I'd say bet."

"Mm-hmm. Guess you owe me one." I give him a wink, then quickly let Sassy outside before we leave.

Jerry and Belinda got hitched last weekend and are having a party to celebrate their nuptials today. I can't believe they got engaged just four months ago, and it's already April. Though Tyler has known about Archer and me for almost a month, it's the first time everyone will *see* us together as a couple. When we're in the car, I let out a sigh and grin.

"What's up?" he asks as we head that way.

"I'm just a tad nervous for Tyler to see us *together*, I guess."

"It's normal to feel nervous. I was too when you met

Annie, but she loves you," Archer admits. "Also, if I want to hold your hand or kiss you, now I can. It's a relief not to have to hide how much I love you."

"You're right. And there's no more fighting the urge to grab your ass anymore," I tell him.

"You wouldn't dare." He tilts his head at me, and I pinch my fingers toward him.

When we arrive at Jerry and Belinda's, so many people are already at their house that we have to park a few blocks down. Archer grabs my hand as we make our way to the front door.

"Ready for the show of a lifetime?" He gives me a wink and rings the doorbell.

"The way I feel about you isn't a show, Archer. We've got the real deal."

"You're absolutely right, sweetheart." He steals a kiss right as the door swings open. Belinda's wearing a tiara with a beautiful and simple white dress that falls to her knees.

"There's the beautiful bride," I sing-song. Archer and I take turns hugging her.

"Hope your sweet tooth is ready. Might've gone a *little* overboard on the pies and cakes." She beams.

"I'm more than ready," I admit, never one to turn down her food.

We find Gemma and Tyler sitting on the couch with sweets piled on their plates. As soon as Gemma sees us together, her face breaks into a wide smile. Tyler gives Archer a head nod.

Jerry's happily holding Scarlett as he chats with Noah and Katie. Half the town is here along with the cooks and servers from the deli. The house is packed.

"Want to grab some food?" Archer asks, then leads me into the kitchen. I pull him close, sliding my tongue between his lips and not giving a shit who sees.

A clearing of a throat behind us pulls us apart. Tyler's standing behind Archer with his arms crossed, but he's not mad.

"So, should I be expecting a wedding invite soon?" he taunts, filling his cup full of Belinda's famous pineapple punch.

"What if we're already married?" I ask with amusement, giving him an evil eye. "It's funny because you don't know if it's true or not, and considering you did it to me, you'd deserve it."

Tyler scoffs. "Okay, but there was a very good reason for that."

"Yeah, but I haven't forgotten," I remind him.

"Archer wouldn't propose without asking me first. So, you should sleep well at night knowing that I'll know about your engagement before you do," he teases, and I groan at the accuracy.

"He does have a point," Archer says, and I smack him.

"Whose side are you on?" I try to escape him, but he snakes his arm around my waist and pulls me closer.

"*Yours*," he whispers in my ear.

"Just glad you two aren't still sneaking around like we're all stupid or something." Tyler gives me a pointed look. "And I'm leaving before you give me any details."

I snicker, then shrug because I love watching him squirm.

Archer and I grab plates, then find all the pies and cakes. "Wow. Belinda wasn't joking."

I notice the island is full of brownies and cookie squares too.

"I might gain ten pounds today." Archer takes little pieces of everything.

"Oh, you *have* to try this." I point at the whipped cream concoction. "It's Southern coconut cream pie."

"A delicacy?"

"An absolute must-have," I say, grabbing the knife and cutting us both a slice. "Gotta say, I'm glad we didn't eat beforehand because I plan to try everything."

Katie, Noah, Gemma, Tyler, Lexie, and her husband, Brett, are sitting at the dining room table, and we join them, taking the last two chairs. Archer rests his hand on the inside of my thigh, and I love the way it feels.

When I look over at him, I smirk as I take a bite of the coconut pie.

"This is orgasmic," I say, holding back a moan.

Lexie snorts. "It really is. Pretty sure it got me pregnant."

Her mother-in-law turns and raises her brows with a disapproving glare before going back to her conversation with Belinda. Immediately, Lexie sinks back into her seat, and Brett excuses himself.

"Don't worry about her," I offer, knowing how evil the woman can be.

She lowers her voice. "Oh, I'm not. Pretty sure she won't be happy until I give her a grandchild."

"Babies don't fix problems," Katie interjects with truth in her voice. Truth that she knows from personal experience.

"Thanks, y'all." Lexie leans in. "So, how's the dating life going?"

Archer grins. "Great. I'm a five-star catch."

"And I'm the best lay he's ever had," I add.

Lexie bursts out laughing. "Sounds like a match made in heaven."

Archer leans into my ear. "You really are," he admits with a wink.

"Do I hear wedding bells?" Noah offers.

"Your own," I retort.

"Aunt Everleigh, I'll marry you." Owen runs over, carrying a huge slice of strawberry cake.

"Aw, sweetie. Well, I'll tell ya what. In fifteen years, if I don't have a ring on my finger yet, then it's an automatic yes. But trust me when I say you're gonna find someone closer to your age before that happens."

"Don't give me a heart attack." Katie holds her hand over her heart. "Owen, you're not allowed to date ever."

"I already am, Mom."

Her eyes nearly bug out of her head. "Since when? You're eleven!"

"Two weeks ago. Dad knows." Owen throws Noah under the bus without a second thought, and we all laugh.

A few of the older women who come into the shop notice how I am around Archer, and I know it's only a matter of time before it spreads all over town.

Scarlett begins crying, and Tyler stands to grab her from Jerry. "She might've pooped," Jerry whispers.

Tyler chuckles, then makes a face. "Yeah, I think you're right."

"Do you want me to take care of it?" Gemma asks.

"Nah, I got it, babe. Finish your food."

When he's out of sight, Gemma leans in. "Sometimes, he still gags. It's hilarious because, at this point, I'm completely immune."

"Looking forward to my superhero skill of smelling shit and not throwing up," I say with a laugh.

"You heard it from the lady herself, Archer. The rest is up to you," Katie says, and Noah chuckles.

My cheeks heat as Archer squeezes my thigh again.

He smirks. "Might be able to make that happen."

"Oh my God. If it were up to all of you, I'd be pregnant before the end of the year," I exclaim.

"Would that be a bad thing?" Archer asks, and I contemplate his question.

"You're pregnant?" Tyler exclaims when he returns, holding a freshly changed Scarlett. Belinda swipes her from his arms.

"No!" I blurt out. "That's how rumors get started!" I look around the room, repeating myself to make sure everyone hears my answer. Though it might still spread around, it's a rumor I wouldn't mind. Archer would make a great dad, and if I'd like to eventually have kids with someone, it'd no doubt be him.

The subject is changed, and Archer leans in and whispers in my ear, "You're blushing."

I grin and lick my lips. "And it's all because of you."

Monday morning comes quickly, and I couldn't be happier to be at work. Sure, sometimes it's so busy I don't have time to think, but I love it. If I've learned anything while being on bedrest, it's how much I enjoy my job. Not being at the boutique was pure torture.

After I open the shop, customers flood in as usual. A few more months are left until summer arrives, but it's already starting to get hotter outside. Right now, the store is still covered in pastel-colored clothes, but in a few weeks, it will be full of colorful neons.

Before lunch, we get a quick break, and it gives me a chance to chat with Dana. It's been a while since just the two of us have worked together.

We start folding a pile of crumpled shirts, and I take the opportunity to ask questions. "How have you been lately?"

"I've been doing great. Reading a lot. Hanging out with my new roommate."

"Oh, you found someone to finally move in?"

She smiles, but it doesn't quite meet her eyes. "Yeah, it was by luck, honestly."

"I bet you're relieved. I know you've been looking for someone for a few months."

"I was. She was in the area looking for a place to stay and ran into me. Sometimes, it's like the universe puts people in your life for a reason, ya know?"

I nod, then walk over to a rack and re-clip some pants that were hanging haphazardly. Though we're chatting, there's a weird vibe in the room that I can't seem to place. It's been like this ever since the night of Archer's party at the bar, but it could also be my anxiety.

Since the accident, I've been suspicious of everything and everyone.

Granted, I shouldn't have embarrassed her the way I did. Between the alcohol and my jealousy, I should apologize, but it happened so long ago that I wonder if it's worth it. So I awkwardly keep it inside and try to keep the conversation going.

Checking the time, I realize it's almost eleven. "You can head out for lunch if you'd like. I'm meeting Gemma and Katie in an hour."

She gives me a nod. "Sounds good. I won't be long."

Dana walks to the back, and I hear her punch buttons on the microwave.

While I have some alone time, I pull out my phone and text Archer.

Everleigh: Miss you! Love you.

A minute passes, and my phone buzzes.

Archer: Miss and love you more.

Everleigh: Loved you first.

Archer: Bullshit.

I chuckle and finish cleaning the store before the midday crowd arrives. After I've resituated the front displays, a few people walk in.

"Everleigh," Mrs. Letto says. "Do you have any of those leggings with the pockets? My granddaughter was telling me about them."

I grin. "Yep, right over here."

She runs her hand across the material. "Oh wow. These feel like a baby's bottom. Super soft."

"You'll never wanna take them off," I express. She goes through the rack and chooses one of each color. When Dana returns from her break, I check the time and realize I need to get going so I'm not late. I ring up those who are ready, then grab my purse.

"If you need any help, please text me," I tell Dana, and she gives me a small wave.

"I will," she says, but it's clipped like she's annoyed.

The sky looks dark in the distance, like the bottom's going to fall out at any moment, so I decide to drive instead of walk.

It only takes a few minutes to get there, and I parallel park across the street from the deli. I make sure to position my self-defense keychain where the pepper spray is comfortable in my hand before getting out. Honestly, I feel kinda stupid being so paranoid, but I'd rather be safe than sorry.

As I make my way toward the front door, I see Katie and Gemma sitting in the booth by the window. They wave at me, and Katie glances down at her watch, shocked.

When I walk in, they give me shit for being on time.

"I can't win here! So I guess that means you two are buying *me* lunch today?"

"Meh." Gemma shrugs. "We didn't bet this time."

"What? I should've dragged my ass gettin' here."

Our server arrives to take our order, then brings us our drinks.

"Sooooo…" Katie says, waggling her brows at me. "I want the scoop. Ring or positive pregnancy test yet?"

"Yeah, am I gonna be a bridesmaid or auntie first?" Gemma asks.

I roll my eyes with a groan and laugh. "Y'all are lucky you didn't scare him away with all that talk. I thought for sure he'd wanna run, but everything's perfect. I guess he's one of those rare kinds who doesn't throw up by talkin' about the future.

And I do mean *future*." I glare at them both to start
tight-lipping it.

"Oh c'mon. You two looked happy on Saturday. It's
obvious how much Archer cares about you," Katie says. "I'm
lovin' it for you."

I bite my lower lip, remembering the very dirty things he
did to me that night. "I am too."

I meet Gemma's eyes. "How did Tyler *really* react to the
news?"

"Truthfully?" She raises a brow.

I nod, though I'm nervous about what she's going to say.

"He said he had already figured it out. I think the birthday
party sealed the deal."

"What? How? We hadn't even done the deed yet!"

She shrugs. "He said it was painfully obvious. The
chemistry between you two is undeniable, Ev. You don't have
to have sex for everyone to see it."

I laugh. "I guess you're right. Did he say anything else?"

"Well, he did mention that if Archer breaks your heart, he's
going to fire him, then kick his ass."

"Figures," I say.

At the same time, Katie mutters, "Geez. What if Everleigh's
the one who breaks Archer's heart?"

I snort. "Are you kidding me? The man makes me come in
record time *and* cooks for me. Don't be surprised if I'm the one
who proposes to him someday."

Gemma snickers. "So it's going good-*good*."

I release a breathy sigh. "*Amazing.* Mind-blowing.
Honestly, he treats me like a queen, which is something I've
never experienced before. I always come first, figuratively and
literally—usually a few times too. It's nice to be with a man
who worships me in and out of the bedroom, ya know? It's a

new concept to me, and I wouldn't do anything to fuck that up, at least not intentionally."

"I'm sure you won't, but it's about damn time you settled down. I was worried you'd be fluttering around like a butterfly until you're fifty. Not that there's anything wrong with that, but I knew deep down you wanted a relationship with substance."

"I didn't realize how much I needed stability in a man until now. Can't believe it took me this long actually," I admit.

"You were just waitin' for the right man," Katie says, sipping her sweet tea.

"Very true. And his sister and niece are super sweet. I honestly wished Annie lived here because you two would love her so much. She'd totally be a part of our girl gang. Also, Sadie is the cutest kid. She's only five but way too smart for her own good."

Katie laughs. "Most kids are. Owen is like that too. The things they can do online amazes me."

"How is my favorite little man doing? " I ask.

"Apparently, he really *does* have a girlfriend. Like what the hell? I'm too young to worry about him dating already."

"I heard Owen say Noah knew. Was that true?" Gemma asks.

"Yes, and apparently, Noah's been giving him pointers on how to treat girls." She groans. " Noah acts like he was some ladies' man or something when it took him a decade to confess his undying love to me."

We giggle and chat, and it's just what I needed today. When our food arrives, Gemma changes the subject.

"How've you been feeling lately? Still sore and achy?"

"Mostly back to normal. I have a wicked battle wound, something I'll have to share with my future kids. Like, don't mess with your mom because she got stabbed and lived to tell the tale. Took a knife right to the gut."

Gemma snorts. "Oh my God. That's terrible, but it does make you sound like a badass."

"'Cause I am." I take my keychain off my purse and flick open the small key knife.

Katie grins. "Well, if the boutique doesn't work out for you, maybe you should teach self-defense for women at the gym."

"Nah, I'd probably make more money stripping. Apparently, I have really nice tits," I whisper, giving Katie a wink.

"It's the shock value for me," Gemma says. "I honestly never know what's going to come out of your mouth."

"And trust me when I say I love keeping you on your toes. But anyway, enough about me. How's the wedding planning going?"

Katie beams as she gushes. "It's stressful but exciting all at the same time. We picked out the cake and flowers. Finally have the invitations, which means I'll be busy sending those soon. And we also booked the Magnolia Springs Bed and Breakfast for the wedding night. My mom is over the moon excited."

"I bet she is," Gemma says. "I can't wait. I'm so happy for you two to finally tie the knot. I mean, you're already practically married, but still. It's gonna be a gorgeous day."

"No, we basically are at this point," Katie agrees. "We go back and forth about what to eat for dinner almost every single night. When neither of us can decide, we make Owen pick. If that's not marriage, I don't know what is."

I chuckle, taking a bite of my sandwich.

"I love him, though. I feel like I'm finally living the life I always dreamed of having. Noah's such a wonderful dad to Owen and the twins. All four of us are so damn lucky."

"You really are," I say. "You both are living a fairy tale."

"You are too," Katie says, and Gemma agrees.

"Not gonna lie, though, the chase in the beginning is the best part. The random sex in the back of the car, on the counter, in the shower, and—"

"Okay, that's enough," I interrupt. "Don't want to hear about my brother's sexcapades." I pretend to throw up in my mouth and change the topic. "How's my sweet little niece?"

"Scarlett's getting big. She crawls everywhere and babbles all day long. I have a feeling that when she can speak full sentences, she's going to talk my ear off. Pretty sure she got the same Blackwood gene as you, Ev."

My head falls back in a roar of laughter. "Even I wouldn't wish that upon you. But if that's the case, I'll say a prayer for you 'cause that girl is gonna be a handful."

Gemma sighs. "Tyler will literally blow a gasket if she puts him through half the things you did."

"She could be worse than Everleigh," Katie says. "She has Blackwood *and* Reid genes."

"Oh hell no," Gemma mutters, shaking her head.

"Better start making her a brother or sister now," I suggest. "She'll need someone to keep her straight or be the older sibling to bail the younger one out. No telling what trouble I would've gotten into without Tyler hounding me."

"You mean, how much *more* trouble you would've gotten into?" Gemma mocks.

"True story," I say.

"It's times like this that I'm glad I have all boys," Katie teases, sipping her drink. "I could've had a mini Everleigh, and Lord help all of us if that had happened."

"You still can." I waggle my brows.

When we're done eating, Gemma snatches up the check. Katie protests, but I know it's a losing battle, so I don't even try to argue.

"Thanks, babe," I say after she pays. When we stand, I give them both hugs. "Can we do this again soon?"

"Absolutely," Katie says, then we walk outside.

The clouds are rolling in, and I wave goodbye to Gemma and Katie as they go in the opposite direction. I pull out my phone and call Archer as I head down the sidewalk. My heart is full, and there's a wide smile on my face. Hanging out with my friends is exactly what I needed.

"Hey, baby," he answers.

"Hey! Just finished eating at the deli. How's your day goin' so far?"

"Just fine. How was your lunch?" he asks while I cross the street.

I hear tires squealing, and when I look over, my adrenaline rushes and heart pounds.

"Oh my fucking God," I mutter. "The Escalade…" I barely get out the words as the SUV speeds toward me.

I scream as I try to move from the middle of the road. Everything seems to happen in slow motion before I trip and fall.

CHAPTER EIGHT

ARCHER

I TAKE my lunch break and walk toward the boutique, ready to surprise her with a kiss in the parking lot. I stare up at the sky and hope it doesn't start raining.

As I'm walking and chatting with Everleigh on the phone, I notice her tone change.

"Oh my fucking God," she mutters, then continues, "the Escalade..."

At first, I feel as if I'm living in a nightmare when I hear an engine revving and tires squealing in the distance. Everleigh's screams fill my ear, and then the line goes completely silent. A crashing metal sound bounces against the buildings, and I burst into a full sprint toward the deli.

No, no, no.

My mind races, and I'm not sure I can handle Everleigh getting hurt again. Every fucking terrible scenario fills my mind, and it's torture as I run the few blocks toward her. When I see Everleigh lying on the ground, I think the absolute worst has happened.

My body goes into autopilot. I can't think about anything

other than getting to her and making sure she's okay. I pick up my pace, running faster than I've ever run before.

People rush out of the deli as smoke escapes the hood of the SUV.

"Did anyone call 911?" I shout over the chatter of the witnesses to the accident. After pushing through the horde of people on the street and sidewalk, I bend down to help her up and feel a bit of relief when I realize she's conscious.

"Baby." I steady her and force her to look into my eyes. "Are you okay?"

She breathes out and nods. Bending over, she picks up her purse and phone from the pavement. "It happened so fast. I saw it come toward me, so I ran. Then I tripped and fell, but I managed to get back to my feet before it could hit me. Holy shit. It's—"

She slurs some of her words as shock takes over.

"Are you hurt?" I examine her body, looking for blood.

"No, no, I'm fine. I think," she says, looking down at the road rash on her palms. It pisses me off that she's going to have to suffer from this now too.

"Is it on fire?" a woman asks as sizzling sounds come from the Escalade. It sideswiped at least four cars before it crashed into a pole.

"It's gonna explode!" someone shouts when smoke billows out.

Everleigh and I walk closer to see who's driving. Two men surround the door and try to open it. It looks like the airbags have deployed, but the whole front is bashed in. A screeching sound echoes out as the door is forcefully pulled open.

They help a woman step out, who then pushes them away when she stumbles to her feet. Her face is bloody from the shattered glass. Though her red hair is messy, I get a flash of recognition.

It's *her*—the woman who attacked Everleigh.

"You fuckin' bitch," she screams in a high-pitched tone. Her eyes are just as crazed as before. "You skank! You deserve to be dead because you're the reason my husband is no longer alive!"

That's all the confirmation I need to know that this is Natasha, Eric's wife. We all assumed right.

I move Everleigh behind me, trying to block her from this psychopath.

"You deserve to feel the same pain I felt the night I learned he was gone," she yells. With the large crowd surrounding us, it becomes more of a showdown than anything.

Someone tries to grab Natasha's arm, but she yanks it away. "Don't fucking touch me!"

"You deserve to be in jail," I hiss.

"And that slut deserves to be dead!"

Gasps are heard all around.

"You're insane, Natasha!" Everleigh shouts. "I didn't know he was married!" Everleigh's body trembles against me.

"Yes, you did," she seethes. "You're a goddamn liar!"

"I'm not lying. It was a fling, and it would've never happened had he told me he had a wife," Everleigh tells her, but there's no way she'll ever convince Natasha otherwise.

It all happens so quickly. Natasha reaches behind her and pulls a gun from the back of her pants. The crowd gasps, then disperses. I swallow hard, guarding Everleigh with my body. If she wants to shoot her, she'll have to go through me first, but I'm not about to let that happen.

"*Natasha…*" I say, holding out my hands. "Put the gun down."

"Move out of the fucking way," she says between gritted teeth. "This is between me and that whore."

"You don't want to do this. Set it down before you hurt someone."

Natasha moves forward until she's standing three feet away. I reach behind me, holding Everleigh in place.

"Get out of the goddamn way," she says at the top of her lungs, her voice echoing off the downtown buildings.

I blink and feel Everleigh slip out from behind me. There's a noise, and seconds later, Natasha's legs are buckling from under her. She falls to the ground, and I turn to see Everleigh with nostrils flared, holding a Taser. Her hands are shaking, and I know she's unsettled by the expression on her face.

Before I can move forward, Tyler comes out of nowhere and kicks the gun away. It all happens so quickly that even I'm stunned at how fast Natasha went down.

Tyler wraps his arm around Everleigh. She immediately drops the Taser, and I see the darts buried in Natasha's skin. The woman is on the ground, hissing out in pain, and when she tries to move, no one moves forward to help her. Sirens blare in the distance, and within a few minutes, the police are on the scene.

A few officers and EMTs surround us. Tyler informs them that Natasha is the one who held us at gunpoint. They help her onto a gurney and let her know she'll be cuffed as they bring her to the hospital. She's banged up, but honestly, the woman needs some mental help. She doesn't say a word as she glares at us.

After they wheel her to the back of an ambulance, I focus on Everleigh and hear Tyler scolding her. "You did a good thing, but you should *never* tase someone who's got a finger on the trigger of a gun! She could have shot you guys."

"I know, but I panicked," she says with tears in her eyes as the reality of what happened caught up with her. "I didn't know what else to do. I was so fucking scared. Thank God it worked, and you're alive." She meets my eyes, then pulls me into her arms.

Her body shakes, and I kiss her hair, trying to soothe her. "Thank God we both are."

Officer Proctor walks through the crowd, then over to us. "You're both very lucky," he states. "One of the callers said Everleigh almost got run over, and then the driver whipped out a gun. I'm assuming she knows you personally?""

Everleigh nods, and I speak up. "She's the one who stabbed her too. I recognized her face. She's also driving the same vehicle that was following us."

As Everleigh tells him every detail of what happened, the officer jots notes down on his pad.

"What's going to happen to her?" Everleigh asks once she's done.

"She's going to the hospital, then we'll question her. If she cooperates, we may be able to offer her a lesser sentence. If she doesn't, she could be charged with attempted murder," he states. "Amongst other things, depending on what the prosecutor decides."

Once we're finished talking to Officer Proctor, Gemma and Katie rush over just as shaken up as the rest of us.

"Oh my God, Everleigh." Gemma hugs her, and Katie joins in. "We didn't know what was going on. All of a sudden, we heard the squealing and screaming, then a crowd formed. Once we saw the gun, neither of us knew what to do besides stay put."

"That's good," Everleigh says. "That was the smart thing to

do, considering I think Natasha followed me and was waiting for me to come out."

"I have to go back to work. Dana's running the shop alone, and I've already been gone for two hours." She watches the tow truck hook up to the SUV.

"You should probably call Lexie and see if she can cover for you," I suggest, but she doesn't respond.

"Everleigh. You can't force yourself to work in this condition. You're really shaken up," I finally say, grabbing her car keys.

"She's already done so much for me over the past few months."

"And I'm sure she'll be more than happy to continue to help. Otherwise, close the shop early, but you need to take the rest of the day off."

"Fine," she complies.

Taking her hand, I lead us to her car, then guide her into the passenger side. After she buckles in, Everleigh pulls out her phone. Before I get to the driver's side, Tyler comes over and pulls me into a tight hug.

"Thank you," he tells me. "I could've lost my sister again if it weren't for you."

"I promised I'd take care of her, Tyler. I meant every word."

"I know you did, and I appreciate it so damn much. Also, you should take the rest of the day off and be with her. I'll cancel your afternoon appointments. This is more important."

"I agree," I say.

I get in the car and start the engine but don't drive off yet.

"Lexie's gonna go in. I owe her so fucking much. And you?" She faces me with a look of disbelief. "I owe you everything."

I shake my head. "No, baby. I'm here to protect and love you. It's my honor to keep you safe."

"Archer, you could've been shot today."

"You're right, but I would've taken a bullet for you, Everleigh."

Tears begin to fall down her cheeks. I reach over and pull her into my arms. "Don't cry, sweetheart."

"It's just too much. All of this. I've constantly been looking over my shoulder, waiting for when she'd come after me again. The thought of losing you…"

"Baby, I'm not going anywhere. You're safe. I'm safe. And we're going home to snuggle for the rest of the day."

"That sounds like heaven," she says as I wipe away her tears.

I do a U-turn and drive us home.

When we get inside the house, Everleigh bends down and tightly hugs Sassy. The dog has no idea what's going on and that she almost lost us.

"Babe, you know what sounds nice right now?" I ask, hoping to calm her.

"What's that?"

"A hot bubble bath and a glass of wine."

Her face breaks into a small smile. "I love you more than life itself, Archer Boone. You're seriously my dream come true."

"I could say the same about you, baby. Now go get undressed and start the water. I'll grab the wine."

She nods. "Sounds like a plan."

CHAPTER NINE

EVERLEIGH

BESIDES WINTER, because Christmas is everything, summer is my favorite season. Alabama weather in early May is perfect, and everyone's moods are brighter with the school year ending. Before it gets too hot, I open the boutique doors and bring sales racks of clothes onto the sidewalk. It's the best.

This time, it's even better knowing that Natasha is behind bars. I haven't completely let my guard down because Krystal is still out there somewhere, but the woman who tried to kill me twice is no longer a threat.

After evidence and statements were provided and collected, there was enough to put her away for a while. She was charged with stalking in the first degree and attempted murder. I hope she can get some kind of psychological help since Eric's murder essentially made her snap.

It's been a few weeks since the incident, and besides the threatening messages from Krystal, life has gone back to normal. Archer and I have grown closer than ever, but a few women have still come into the boutique asking about him. But now, I get the pleasure of telling them he's *all mine*. What's even more exciting is attending Katie and Noah's wedding as a couple next month.

Today I've stayed so busy with customers and keeping things stocked that hours pass before I realize what time it is.

Everleigh: Make sure to wash your face after dinner tonight.

Archer: Huh? Why?

"What're you smiling at?" Lexie asks as I read the text on my phone.

"None of your business." I smirk.

"I know a sexting face when I see it."

I roll my eyes, then type out my reply.

Everleigh: Because I like my seat clean.

Archer: Jesus fucking Christ.

My cheeks redden. I can imagine his deep, gravelly voice saying those words to me right now.

"Yep, totally sexting," Lexie sing-songs.

"I can't help it. I miss him during the day," I admit, grabbing a few pairs of jeans to refold.

"You live in the same house and see each other when you're not working," she reminds me. "Missing one another is good for a relationship. If I saw Brett too much, I would've been sick of him within the first six months."

I burst out laughing, knowing she's not joking. They have a solid marriage but were high school sweethearts, so their honeymoon phase ended years ago.

Dana shows up for her afternoon shift, and the three of us work effortlessly to keep things running smoothly. Most of the time, Dana keeps to herself, which doesn't bother me. Since my employees have been working so hard, I invite them out for drinks, my treat. Being together outside of the store is good for morale and team building.

"So, I spoke with Heidi, and she said she can meet us for drinks tomorrow night after the boutique closes. You guys in?" I ask Lexie and Dana.

"Hell yes!" Lexie immediately responds.

"I have plans with my new roommate," Dana says.

"New roommate? Who?" Lexie asks.

"She's not a local. Y'all wouldn't know her."

"Well, she's welcome to join us," I offer. "The more, the merrier!"

"Yeah, I'd love to meet her," Lexie adds.

Dana nervously licks her lips as if she's searching for an excuse. Lately, she's been more distant than usual, and it's one of the reasons I wanted the four of us to get together.

"My roommate is an introvert and doesn't like to be around a lot of people. She's hiding from her ex-husband and is weird about letting anyone see her. It's for her protection," Dana explains, and Lexie gives me a look that says Dana's full of shit.

"Oh wow, is she in some kind of danger?" I ask genuinely.

"No, I don't think so. She's really quiet and prefers to be around people she knows and trusts."

The weirdness of this conversation has me narrowing my eyes. Either Dana's hiding a fugitive or she's making this story up to avoid hanging out.

"Alright, well, if she decides she wants out of the house, she's welcome to come have a drink with us," I offer politely.

"I'll let her know, thanks."

After that, Dana spends the next hour working as far away from the two of us as possible. The way Lexie's acting tells me we'll be talking about this tomorrow night.

As I get ready to leave, I open Archer's text, and his palm wrapped around his thick cock comes into view with the message, *Waiting at home for you.*

Before I have a chance to lock the screen, Lexie gasps next to me.

"Was that a dick pic?" she whispers, then elbows me in the side.

"Please tell me you didn't see that." I cringe at the thought of my employee seeing Archer's goods.

"Oh, honey. I saw it. Inspiring me to go home to my man right now."

I snort, shaking my head. "Tell Brett he can thank me later."

"I'm not stupid enough to tell him that, please. It's not good for his ego."

Laughing, I walk toward the front door. "Bye now!"

As soon as I'm on the sidewalk, I call Archer.

"Hey," he answers.

"Don't hey me! You sent me a dirty pic!"

"Yeah. Did you like it?" I hear the amusement in his tone.

"Yeah, and so did Lexie."

"You showed her?"

"No! She just happened to be next to me and peeked over. Gave her a show."

"Great. I won't be able to look her in the eyes now."

I chuckle, getting into my car and starting the engine. "Probably not, but you better have it ready for me in about five minutes when I get home."

"Deal."

As soon as I walk in, Sassy greets me, and I give her some attention before I find Archer in the kitchen—stripped down to his boxers.

"Are you serious?"

I gaze down his body and stop on the bulge between his legs.

"I thought you'd be hungry after work, so I started making burgers. Do we have any cheese?"

"You're talking about food when you're practically naked and hard?" I playfully shout, kicking off my shoes, then pulling off my shirt.

He raises a brow, admiring my black bra and licking his lips. "Payback, sweetheart."

I gasp, unzipping my jeans and tearing them off next. "For what?"

He smirks while coming closer, then wraps his arms around my hips. "You've been driving me crazy all damn day. After your first message, I had to spend thirty minutes with a nineteen-year-old who nearly kicked my ass because I couldn't focus."

"So, you're just going to tease me through dinner?" I stick out my lower lip, and he captures it with his teeth.

"Yep. I'll have it done in just a few minutes."

My shoulders slump. "Rude."

He swats my ass, then goes back to the stove. I grab the cheddar from the fridge and set it on the countertop, then go freshen up.

"So I'm meeting Lexie and Heidi for drinks tomorrow night after we close. We need a chance to discuss some work stuff outside of the shop. You're welcome to join if you want, but just know it'll consist mostly of girl talk."

He chuckles. "Yeah, that sounds like a fun time *for you*. I'm gonna pass, but thanks for the invite."

"Maybe Tyler or Noah can meet you there too?"

"Nah, that's okay. They're busy with work and family stuff. Sassy and I will hold down the fort. Just let me know when you leave so I can pick you up. Wait, how come Dana isn't going?"

I repeat her words from earlier along with my suspicions.

"You could be paranoid with everything that's happened. Maybe her roommate really *is* trying to lay low and hide."

I shrug, still having my doubts. "Maybe, but Dana's also been acting weird, so I think it's something else."

We finish our food and cuddle on the couch with Sassy on the floor next to us. I never thought this would be my life—being serious with a man who lives with me, casually sharing meals together, and watching TV until bedtime.

I didn't know I wanted or needed this until Archer. Maybe it took meeting the right guy—one who'd take a bullet for me without thinking twice.

"Hey, ladies. Whatcha having tonight?" Damien asks as the three of us approach the bar.

"Vodka soda, two Jack and Cokes, and three tequila shots,"

I respond, setting my card on the counter. "Start us a tab, please."

He smiles wide as he grabs it, then makes our drinks. Lexie, Heidi, and I find a high top table near the back of the bar and wait for them to be delivered.

"So I told Heidi what Dana said and how weird she's been acting. She has a theory," Lexie says.

"Ooh, tell me," I blurt out. While I shouldn't be gossiping about one of my employees, I'm making an exception this time. Considering what's happened to me, I'd rather be in the know.

"Last week, she mentioned driving her roommate to the airport and then picking her up the next day. She stumbled to come up with a reason when I asked about the quick trip, which made me think she was lying. She said her roommate had to meet a lawyer and only wanted to stay one night."

"Couldn't she just have met with him on FaceTime or over the phone? That seems excessive to have to fly back and forth?" Lexie states.

"Yeah, unless she had to sign papers or make a cash payment. Plausible if her intentions are to stay on the down low," I suggest.

"Maybe she's in the witness protection program," Heidi says. "And maybe Dana's hosting her until she goes to her final destination."

"Oh my God, we've all been watching too much Crime TV." I burst out laughing.

"What's so funny?" Damien asks with our drinks in hand.

"You don't even wanna know," Lexie tells him, grabbing her vodka soda.

"Thanks," I say, reaching for the shots and handing them out.

Once Damien leaves, we hold up our glasses. "Alright, what should we drink to?"

"To Dana's roommate," Lexie cheers.

Heidi giggles and adds, "To Blair, then."

Lexie and I snap our gazes to Heidi. "Her name is Blair?" I ask.

"Yeah, that's what she told me anyway." Heidi shrugs.

"Now I'm convinced she's a witch," Lexie says.

The three of us laugh, clink our glasses, and shoot back the tequila.

For the next few hours, we talk about the boutique, creative display ideas, and upcoming launches. I love adding jewelry and accessories from other small businesses too. I'd much rather buy from them than a corporation.

"Oh my gosh, you look like my man," I slur when Archer appears at the table. "You comin' to give me a ride?"

He fights back a grin and keeps his stance. "Yep. You ready?"

"Archer!" Lexie and Heidi cheer loudly when they realize it's him.

"*Shhh*…he's in the witness protection program," I whisper-shout.

Archer gives me a funny look as the girls giggle.

"Huh?"

"You need a new identity," I tell him seriously. "Hmm… how about Fabio Bigg Schlong."

He pops a brow, confused, then just shakes his head. "Alright, sure. It's time to go home, baby."

I frown, then finish my drink. "Fine."

"Do you ladies need a ride home?" Archer asks.

"No, Brett should be here any minute. He's taking Heidi home too," Lexie slurs.

The moment I try to stand and miss Archer's hand, then nearly face-plant on the floor is when I realize I've had too much.

"Jesus. You okay?" Archer grabs my waist, holding me up.

I blink hard, waiting for the ground to stop moving. "Perfectly great."

Archer chuckles. I say good night to everyone, then wait while Archer closes the tab.

"Bye, Damien!" I shout. "Thanks for the booze."

He flashes a small smirk, then waves, keeping his attention on Archer.

"Is there a beef between you two?" I ask after he buckles me in.

"No, why?"

"He had a *look*."

Archer furrows his brows, then walks around the car and slides into the driver's seat. "Well, he came in for a session last week. First *and* last."

"What happened?"

Archer drives us home, and the realization that I haven't eaten hits me.

"Nothing."

"Archer," I slur, fighting to keep my eyes open. "Tell me."

"He made an offhanded comment, and when we were training, I swung a little too hard."

I gasp at the realization. "You gave him that black eye!"

I hadn't noticed until he gave us our second round. Lexie asked about it, and he shrugged with a smug grin.

"Trust me, it was well-deserved."

"What'd he say?" I demand. "Don't lie to me either."

He flashes me a look that says he doesn't want to tell me,

then inhales sharply as his shoulders slump. "He made a sexual comment about Gemma."

My jaw drops. "No way! How stupid are you to do that about the owner's wife?"

"Exactly. I told him as much too. He kept going, and when he mentioned her ass, I lost it. Whipped off my gloves and punched him in the face."

Archer parks in the driveway and turns off the car. "Tyler freaked out, but once I told him why, he understood, then banned Damien from the gym."

"Good. Geez. But wait, how come you didn't tell me about that?"

"Tyler didn't want Gemma to know and asked me not to tell you because he knows you'd slip."

"That little shit!" I scowl.

Archer chuckles, gets out, and meets me at my door.

"Well, is he wrong?" he asks, holding out his hand.

"Shush." I take it, and he helps me stand. "I probably would've in a *look how hot you are after having a baby* kind of statement."

"I'm surprised Damien didn't tell you."

"Me too," I say honestly.

Archer leads us inside the house, and I find Sassy passed out on the couch. There's an empty bowl on the coffee table, and I smile at the thought of Archer and Sassy sharing popcorn.

"Probably didn't want you to do the same to the other eye." I snort.

"If he knows what's good for him, he won't talk about another man's woman again." He wraps his arms around me and pulls me to his chest. "Especially my woman."

I stand on my tiptoes and press my lips to his. "Oh yeah?"

He smacks my ass, then lifts me until my legs circle his waist.

"Yep. Hope you're sober enough to feel what I'm about to do to you."

My eyes widen in shock. He normally denies me when I've had too much to drink because I can get a little mouthy and wild. But as soon as he strips me out of my clothes and gives me my first orgasm of the night, I'm not complaining one bit.

CHAPTER TEN

ARCHER

"You hit like a kid," I say when Kyle swings at me and misses. He's around seventeen and a cocky little shit. Too bad he doesn't have the moves to back up his ego.

He circles me, but I don't flinch.

"I bet I could knock you out," he retorts.

"Dude, I've been waiting thirty minutes. Make your move." I keep my defensive stance and watch him closely.

He aims for my face again, but I block him. Next, he swings an uppercut to my jaw, but I hardly flinch.

"Put some power into your punches," I direct. "You have the positions down but no confidence. You chicken out as soon as you—"

Before I can finish my sentence, Kyle fakes a punch, and as I dodge it, he kicks my knee and forces me down. Instinctively, I hold up my hands to cover my face, but Kyle's in too much shock to react. I kick out my leg and take him down with me.

"About time a fire gets lit under your ass." I chuckle as he lies flat on his back. "Nice job. Once your opponent is down, keep them down. Aim for the face and gut, but keep watch so they don't take you out. You hesitated after the fact."

I get to my feet and hold out my hand to help him up. "But you did a good job."

"Thanks. See ya next week?" he asks, ripping off his gloves with a cheesy grin.

"Yep. Nice work. See ya then."

After I clean up, I order a protein berry blast from the smoothie bar. Tyler finds me shortly after and asks how things are going.

"Great, can't complain honestly."

"I'm glad to hear it. Can you believe this time last year we could only talk on the phone a couple of times a month?"

"It's surreal. I've only been out for six months, but so much has happened during that time. My life has changed more than I thought was possible," I admit. One of those life-changing things is Everleigh. I'm so happy and grateful for what we have, yet I can't fight the feeling that I'm going to somehow fuck it up. Maybe it's because I've never been in a serious relationship before or that I just love her so damn much that the fear of losing her consumes me.

"Yeah, after I was released, my world drastically changed too. Gemma and I had to become friends again first, and once I confirmed she still had feelings for me, I knew a life with her here was all I wanted."

I smile as I think about everything he's overcome. He looks at me as if he's waiting for me to say something else, and when I don't, he continues. "I know it's none of my business, but it's been weighing on me, so I have to ask."

"What's up?"

"Do you think you'll stay in Lawton Ridge? Since Annie

and Sadie are in Wyoming, I wasn't sure of your plans, especially now that you're with Everleigh."

Ahh…the long-awaited big brother talk.

"Honestly, I've not thought too far into the future. I enjoy being here, and I love Everleigh. I hope one day Annie and Sadie will move to Alabama, but I think that's gonna take some convincing."

Tyler nods with a grin. "I'd like that for ya, man. Family's important to have around."

"I agree, though I think of you as my family too," I say truthfully. "You gave me a home."

"And I'd do it again, brother." Tyler hugs me before we part ways.

I decide to walk to the grocery store before I head home so I can make Everleigh dinner. She has a few hours left of work, and I'd like to surprise her.

On the way there, I think about my conversation with Tyler and then send Annie a text.

Archer: Things going okay? Notice anything weird again?

Annie: No, not since that one time. Don't worry, I'm keeping an eye out.

I grin because she knew what I was going to say next.

Archer: Okay, good. Can't be too safe. I wish we lived closer.

Annie: Me too. Maybe someday.

I make my way into the store and grab a basket. Next, I find the potatoes, then head toward the meat.

"Oh my gosh, Archer, hi!" I turn and see Dana standing inches from me.

"Hey, how are ya?" I ask politely.

"Great! How 'bout yourself?"

"Can't complain," I say, lowering my eyes to the steaks. "Just grabbing a few things."

"Ooh, meat and potatoes. Yum." She places her hand on my arm. "Everleigh's a lucky woman."

"Uh, thanks." I step back, creating space between us until her hand drops. She ignores my unease.

"So what have you been up to? Training lots of people?"

"Yep, staying busy." I place two ribeyes in my basket.

"It's a real shame Everleigh took you off the market so fast." She inches closer. "But I can't say I blame her." She smirks, and I'm immediately uncomfortable.

Considering this is a small town, people will speculate if we're standing too close. It's enough for me to want to get my ass away from her and out of here.

"Well, I better go if I'm gonna have time to cook. See ya later." I walk away before she says anything else. Not sure what the hell that was about, but I wasn't staying to find out.

When I'm only a few minutes from the house, I get a text. My heart races when I see it's from an unknown number.

I click on it and find a picture of Everleigh with Gemma and Katie. They're sitting together at the deli, and though there's no date on it, I remember the outfit. Everleigh was wearing it the day Natasha nearly ran her over. That was a month ago, so why is Krystal just now sending this?

And does that mean Krystal was here, or is someone else

watching her? Were Natasha and Krystal somehow working together?

A dozen questions run through my mind as I unlock the front door. Sassy greets me, then follows me to the back, where I let her outside. After I set the bag of groceries on the counter, I stare at my phone.

I realize she sent it with a message.

Unknown: It'd be a shame if all three of them got hurt because of something you did.

My blood boils, and I grind my teeth as my finger hovers over the keyboard. I'm tempted as hell to tell her to fuck off, but I don't want her to get pleasure from knowing she gets under my skin. Instead, I pocket my phone and try to breathe.

Not only has she threatened Everleigh and me but now she's bringing our friends into this, and it makes me even more mad. I take a screenshot, email it to my parole officer and the detective, then block the number. If I can show solid proof, then building a case for harassment will be easier if she shows up.

Once I let Sassy back in, I clean up the house a little, then start preparing dinner. I'm so lost in thought that I don't hear Everleigh come in. It's not until she wraps her arms around my waist from behind that I notice.

"Jesus, you scared me," I admit, spinning around to face her.

"You were pretty focused," she says, pressing her lips to mine. "Smells delicious. And I don't just mean the food."

"I was." I grip her hips and pull her in closer. "How was your day?"

"Great. Pretty busy actually. How about you?"

I release her and finish wrapping the potatoes in foil. When the oven beeps, I place them inside.

"Not bad. Was done by three," I tell her. "I also ran into Dana at the store."

"Yeah?" Everleigh opens the fridge and pulls out the butter, sour cream, and steak sauce.

"She acted a little...*weird*."

Everleigh narrows her eyes. "What do you mean?"

I explain what happened, down to her touching my arm and being in my personal space. I even mentioned what she said about me no longer being single. Everleigh grinds her teeth like she's ready to take her steak knife and find Dana.

"She's been so damn sketchy lately, but this is her final straw. I'm firing her ass tomorrow," she scoffs.

"Babe, don't make any rash decisions. Maybe she was just being friendly, and I took it the wrong way. I'm not Southern bred."

She rolls her eyes. "You don't need to be. Everyone knows there's a fine line between friendly and tryin' to steal another woman's man. She made you uncomfortable, and that doesn't sit right with me."

I grab her wrist and pull her to my chest. "Even if that was her intention, it'd never work. I'm too madly, crazy, and stupidly in love with *you*."

She sighs, then finally smiles. "Fine, but I'm at least having a chat with her. Make sure she knows I'm aware of what she said to my man. Then if she pisses me off again, she's gone."

I chuckle, then tilt up her chin. "Another reason I adore you so much."

I swipe my tongue between her lips and taste her sweetness.

"Maybe you can *show* me just how much," she taunts.

"Always got your mind in the gutter, don't ya?"

Once our food is ready, we sit on the couch and eat. Everleigh puts on another episode from *Only Murders in the Building*, and I contemplate how I'm going to tell her about the text message and picture I got today.

"This show just gets crazier and crazier," she says when it ends. "Also, that was the best steak and potatoes I've ever had." Everleigh smiles, wrapping her arm around me and colliding her lips to mine. "Thank you."

"I need to tell you something."

She straightens, and that wrinkle between her brows appears. I hate making her worry, but I promised not to keep any secrets from her, good and bad.

"What is it?"

After a moment, I explain what I got from the unknown number. Then I show her the screenshot I saved, and she mutters a few curse words.

"Now that you've given me a description of her, if she comes near me, I'm using my Taser."

"Babe, you can't just tase anyone with jet-black hair."

"Tase first, ask questions later," she counters.

I chuckle, pulling her onto my lap. "She's just trying to intimidate and piss me off, but all it does is bring us closer."

"So what you're saying is, orgasms are the way to get revenge." She pops a brow, rocking her body against mine.

"That's exactly right." I lift my hips and push my bulge into her.

Everleigh moans as she grinds into me, then slowly slides off. I give her a look and ask what she's doing.

"I got a little surprise for you today…" She pulls a small container out of her pocket and pops it open.

"What is that?" I ask hesitantly.

She flashes a wicked grin, then slips something onto her tongue.

"Everleigh…"

She reaches for my zipper and pulls out my cock. I lose all train of thought as she steadily strokes me. Lounging back on the couch, I give her all the access she needs and groan when she slides her tongue around the tip.

"Fuck, baby. That feels so—"

Everleigh wraps her mouth around me, and a gush of cool air hits me.

"Holy shit."

Everleigh continues, stroking and lightly sucking. "You like it?"

"I'm…*conflicted*. What did you just eat?"

"A Listerine strip. When I researched it, they suggested letting it dissolve all the way first and then sucking you off."

"I'm sorry, but did you say you *researched* it? Where?"

She smirks and shrugs. "Reddit."

I chuckle as she resumes her delicious assault on my dick. As I fist a hand in her hair, the intensity builds, and another guttural groan escapes me. The cool air feels strange yet pleasurable, and I kinda like it.

"Shit. You do that so well," I hiss through my teeth. Everleigh sucks me deep and releases with a pop before swirling her tongue along the tip. "I'm so close, baby. Remove your shirt," I demand.

Everleigh whips it off, and I lick my lips, thinking about tasting her nipples. "So beautiful."

She increases the pace, her hand twisting up and down my cock, and soon my balls tighten. Everleigh re-positions herself on her knees as I moan out my release. I spill all over her creamy breasts and watch in delight as she licks some off her finger.

"You're naughty as hell," I breathe out. "Can't wait to return the favor."

"Mmm…" She waggles her brows. "Don't threaten me with a good time."

Later that night, after I've given Everleigh three orgasms and snuggled her to sleep, my mind wanders back to the threatening messages. I hate that I'm not only putting Annie and Everleigh at risk but other people I care about too. Tyler knows about Krystal, and I'm sure the others do too, but I'd hate to have to tell them this on top of it. They have kids, and me being here could cause them real harm.

Though I think Krystal is trying to smoke me out, she could be serious. Regardless, I'm not going to cave into the fear because that's exactly what she wants.

As I try to calm down so I can fall asleep, I get a motion alert from one of the cameras. It happens sometimes and usually ends up being a stray cat or squirrel, but it's detected on three of the cameras within seconds.

Quickly, I open up the app to see what caused it, but whatever it was, it seems to be gone. As I check the other cameras just in case, I notice a shadow at the corner of the house moving away, but I can't tell what it was.

I release a deep, ragged breath, and my paranoia kicks in.

Fuck, I'm never gonna sleep now, but I'll hold Everleigh and protect her until the day I die.

CHAPTER ELEVEN

EVERLEIGH

TWO WEEKS LATER

I ROLL OVER IN BED, and Archer's awake, scrolling on his phone. Birds are chirping outside, and the sun is shining through the windows. It looks like it's going to be a beautiful day for Noah and Katie's wedding. I can't believe it's already June.

"We should probably get going," he tells me. "Katie said we needed to be at the chapel before three, and I know you've gotta get dressed."

I groan, snuggling in closer and stealing his warmth. "It's barely ten."

"And I know how much time you need to get ready for big events."

I groan with a sigh. "Fine, you're right. But I have something I need to take care of first." I dip below the covers and between his thighs.

His hand reaches toward me as I peel his boxers down. I

lick from his balls up to the tip before taking him in my mouth. The sound of his groan empowers me. Right now, this man is crumpling under my touch, and I'm living for it. A few seconds later, he's uncovering me as I kiss up his stomach and meet his mouth. With strong hands, he grips my hips, then rips off my panties. The pain mixes with pleasure as I lower myself onto him.

Immediately, our bodies melt together, becoming one. We start slow, kissing and touching each other until our movements grow greedy. A few moments later, Archer rolls me onto my back and secures my wrists above my head.

"Harder," I demand, shoving my heels into his ass. I spread my legs wider and think about how damn grateful I am that this man is mine.

"*Yesyesyes*," I mumble, my muscles tightening as the orgasm threatens to spill over. As soon as he places my nipple in his mouth, I lose control. I squeeze my eyes, my body ready to explode from the intensity streaming through me. It takes everything I have to stay quiet as I ride out the wave, covering my mouth with my hand. The walls at the bed and breakfast are paper thin, and the squeaky springs of the mattress have already given us away. My breasts rise and fall as I try to catch my breath, loving the way his thick cock slides in and out of me.

"You're so goddamn wet," he whispers in my ear.

Archer's movements become more precise as his body trembles. I roll him over and ride him until he groans out his release. I throw my head back and rock my hips as his warmth fills me.

Kissing me gently, Archer wraps his arms around my waist and holds me close. We stay in this position for a minute before cleaning up. Once we're dressed, we head downstairs and eat. The B&B serves breakfast, lunch, and dinner, and I can never pass up a home-cooked meal. I swear it's just as good as Belinda's food.

After we've finished eating, we go upstairs and get ready for the wedding. As of right now, we have over an hour before we have to leave, but luckily, the church isn't too far away.

"I can't get enough of you, baby," he proclaims, leading me into the shower. "Love every damn thing about you."

"I hope not because I'm kinda obsessed with you," I say as we wash up together.

We've been official for four months, and he's become such a major part of my life that I don't know who I am without Archer. He's changed me for the better, which is something I never thought I'd say about a man. Not only has he saved my life more than once but I've fallen head over heels in love with him too. This man is my other half, my best friend, the only person who really knows who I truly am, and I'm *never* giving him up.

"You are stunning, sweetheart." Archer's eyes gaze over my dress once I'm all ready to go.

"You look quite handsome yourself," I say, adjusting his tie. "I can't wait to use this later."

He gives me a wink, and I know if we don't leave, we're going to end up back in bed.

We grab everything we need, then go to the car and head toward the church.

"The last time I wore something like this, I was a teenager."

"We gotta change that. Plan some fancy date nights. You dress like that, then we'll end the night with you licking expensive champagne off my body."

"Damn woman," he mutters, adjusting himself as he focuses on the road. "I love that thought."

"Let's do that sooner than later."

He sets his palm on my thigh, pushing up my dress. Carefully, he peels my panties to the side and runs his fingertips across my clit before dipping two digits inside. With a popped eyebrow, he looks at me. "My wet girl. Stay still."

My head rolls back on my shoulders as I hold his wrist in place. "I love when you touch me," I moan out, arching up toward him. "You know exactly what I need."

"Fuck, baby. Don't make me pull over."

Pulling away, he places his fingers in his mouth and sucks off my juices.

"I wish you would," I whimper, squeezing my legs together.

"Katie would kill me and then you," he contends.

"You're right, she would. I don't want to make her nervous about me showing up late on her wedding day. But thinking about you inside me will be playing in my mind on repeat all evening now."

Archer smirks. "Good. Means I got you right where I want you."

I laugh and glance out the window, noticing the cute shops downtown. Magnolia Springs is one of those absolutely adorable tourist traps, and I understand why Katie loves it so much.

He turns onto the road that leads to the church parking lot. When we get out of the car, a warm breeze brushes against my skin. The weather couldn't have been better, especially considering June is usually so hot.

I turn my head and see the little white church that sits up

on the hill. It's the same place her grandparents got married, and it was Katie's dream to get married here too.

Archer and I walk hand in hand as we make our way to the double doors. There are rooms in the back where we're supposed to meet, and since the place isn't too big, it doesn't take long to find them. As soon as I enter, I spot Katie sitting in a chair getting her hair curled.

"Everleigh," she squeals as I carefully wrap my arms around her. "You're freakin' gorgeous."

"Look at you! Your makeup is perfect, and that tiara looks great on you. You're beautiful," I say, pointing at the jewels. Her hair is in big ringlets that fall past her shoulders.

Gemma comes over and squeezes me. "You made it!"

"Of course! We've been waitin' for this day since high school!" I flash Katie a wink since we all knew Noah was in love with her long before they ever got together.

Katie meets my eyes and sighs. "I've been waiting a lifetime."

"And now the big day is *finally* here," Gemma cheers.

Katie's mother comes in with one of her sisters, and they're each holding one of the twin boys. They bring them over to the couch and sit.

"Oh my gosh! My ovaries! They look so adorable." The twins are dressed in tiny tuxedos.

Leaving over, I kiss their rosy cheeks, happy my lipstick won't easily wipe away. "You both look like mini princes right now."

Owen enters and looks agitated.

"What's wrong?" Katie asks, and he whispers something in her ear.

"I put some in the car. Go ask your dad for the keys," she says, and he leaves.

"Forgot deodorant." She snickers. "Boys."

"At least he thought to ask," Gemma says. "Some of the men at the gym could use that thought process."

Scarlett starts crying, and that's when I notice Belinda sitting in the corner of the room. Gemma rushes over, but I offer to take her. "Hey, sweetie pie. Why so fussy?"

She wraps her arms around me. "You need a nap, huh?"

"Bababa," she demands.

"Mm-hmm. You're right."

Gemma chuckles, handing Scarlett some juice.

"You're gettin' heavy. Gonna be driving soon," I say, adjusting my position.

Gemma shakes her head. "No, I want her to stay this little forever and ever."

"They *never* do," Katie interjects with a sweet smile.

As I keep Scarlett company, Belinda chats with Gemma. When Scarlett tires of me and begins reaching for Belinda, I hand her over.

"We'll be sitting in the front row," Belinda says, taking the diaper bag and walking out.

"They're two peas in a pod." Gemma beams with a sparkle in her eye.

"Tyler told me Belinda's really stepped up as a grandmother," I say.

"She has. Scarlett loves her so much, and Belinda loves to spoil her."

Jerry couldn't have found a better woman to spend the rest of his life with.

After Katie's makeup is done, she stands, then spins so we can see the entire dress.

"Wow," I say just as Katie's mom bursts into tears. "You're stunning."

"My baby is growing up," Mrs. Walker says.

Katie snorts. "Aw, Mama. I've got three babies. I think I'm already grown."

"I know, I know. This just makes it more real."

Luke starts fussing, and Gemma quickly takes him. "I've got it," she says.

"Thank you. The last thing I need is to be puked on."

I chuckle. "Everyone here would understand if you had spit-up on your shoulder."

"Exactly why I kept the guest list very small." Katie winks, and I know how serious she was about inviting only close friends and family. She wanted it to be an intimate moment between her and Noah instead of having a big show for the whole damn town.

After the boys are fed, Katie's mom and aunt make their way out, leaving only Gemma and me with the bride. Katie opens her arms and pulls us into a hug, and that's when I see the tears begin to fall. I pull away and grab a tissue so her mascara doesn't run.

"I love you both so much. Thank you for being the best friends I could ever ask for and sharing today with me," she says.

"You and Noah were always meant to be together," I say. "You were the right one, wrong time kinda country song, and it was destined you'd find your way back to each other."

"I know a thing or two about that, too." Gemma grins. "But yes, I agree!"

Katie sucks in a deep breath as she glances at the clock on the wall. "Guess it's time to go out there, isn't it?"

I nod. "Yes it is, soon-to-be Mrs. Noah Reid."

We head out into the hallway, and as soon as I see Archer, I hook my arm through his. When Noah asked him to be a groomsman a few months ago, Katie took the opportunity to pair us together.

As soon as the music starts, I turn and wink at Katie. "Good luck."

Archer looks at me as I suck in a deep breath. "Ready to go, beautiful?"

"Yep," I say.

About sixty people are in attendance, but only one person here has my full attention. My breath grows ragged as I imagine what it'd feel like to be marrying Archer one day.

As if he has the same thought, he meets my eyes. His Adam's apple bobs as he swallows. "I love you," he whispers. I say it back, and we part ways at the front of the chapel. My gaze stays planted on him until the "Wedding March" begins.

Katie looks like she's floating down the aisle, and everyone's mesmerized by how gorgeous she is. Noah's gaze is focused on her, and it's one of the most magical moments I've ever witnessed.

The pastor steps up, and the ceremony begins. While they each recite the vows they wrote for each other, I glance at Archer and admire how good he looks.

After the pastor pronounces them as husband and wife, Katie and Noah kiss. When they turn around, whistles and cheers fill the room, then the pianist begins playing. After we take pictures with the wedding party and bride and groom, we drive to the event hall for the reception. The guests arrive first, then when Katie and Noah arrive, the real party begins.

Warm rustic lights and white sheers are draped around the room. It has a magical Southern summer feel, and I'm in love with how cozy it is. They're only offering a cocktail hour, finger foods, and dessert bar, then calling it a night after some dancing. I swear, Katie should be an event planner because it's the perfect night.

Archer grabs my hand and pulls me close as we wait in line for drinks. "I think Katie's cousins are eye-fucking you."

I laugh and turn around, noticing some of her distant relatives staring at my ass. "Does that make you jealous?"

He slides his hand down my ass and grabs it. No one sees, but goddamn, I feel it, and I *like* it.

"More like possessive," he growls in my ear, and I smile wide at his tone. Before we get to the front of the bar, I grab his hand, and we slip away down the hallway. I wiggle the doorknob of a closet filled with cleaning supplies and pull him inside. He laughs against my mouth as I lean forward to kiss him.

"What're you doing?" he asks as I unbutton his tux pants and slide them down to his ankles. I pull out his cock and stroke him. I don't even need to answer his question because he knows. After I slip off my panties, he lifts me onto his raging hard-on, then pins me against the door. We're hot and greedy for one another and fucking like we're teenagers.

Right now, all I need is him, just like this.

"You're mine," Archer growls as he bites my neck.

"Good, because you're all mine too. I don't like to share."

"Fuck that, me neither." Our mouths crash together, and our kisses grow more desperate. Moments later, Archer drops to his knees and puts my leg over his shoulder. I hold the top of his head for balance as he licks and sucks my clit, devouring me like a starved man. One finger slides inside and then another as I ride his face, tugging on his hair. I lose myself, nearly forgetting where we are. Brooms fall over, and I'm worried someone will catch us, but at this moment, I don't care.

"Fuck, that feels so good," I groan out. Archer stands and wipes his mouth filled with my juices. He spins me around and presses my hands against the wall. I'm fighting to hold myself up as he fucks me from behind. Our bodies slap together, and I know if he keeps this up, I'm going to come harder than before.

As if he senses I'm close, he reaches around and circles my clit. Within seconds, I unravel again, squirting down his cock.

"Damn, you're so tight," he groans, squeezing my hips with his firm grasp as he loses himself. Once we catch our breaths, I turn around and realize we have made quite the mess.

"You think anyone noticed we were gone?" I ask, ready to collapse on the floor.

"Probably." He shrugs. "Let's find something to clean up before we go back out there."

Archer grabs a paper towel roll and rubs a sheet over my legs, then himself. Next, he helps me move my dress down below my ass, then I adjust his suit jacket and hair. We're a sloppy mess, and it might be more than obvious what we were doing, but I'm not ashamed.

"So you're not giving me my panties back?" I ask before I open the door and check to see if the coast is clear.

"Absolutely not. It's a treasure."

I smirk. "Figured as much. I'll go out first. Give me a few minutes, then meet me at the bar so we don't look suspicious."

"Sounds like a plan," he tells me, pulling me in for one more kiss.

After I leave and shut the door behind me, I make my way down the hallway. The music's blaring so there's no way anyone heard us—*hopefully*.

As soon as I get to the bar, Gemma walks up next to me with a shit-eating grin. "You look guilty as hell."

I shrug and wave her off. "Not sure what you mean."

"So where were you?"

"Studying the inside of a broom closet," I say.

Her head falls back with laughter. "Were you cleaning?" she asks, then fixes my hair.

Leaning in, I whisper, "More like gettin' dirty."

Archer walks up behind me, wrapping an arm over my waist. "Oh, there you are."

Now that we're in the light, I can see how swollen his lips are and know mine probably look the same.

I snort when Gemma shakes her head. "You two need to work on not being so obvious."

Archer choke-laughs at the realization we're busted. Soon, we're grabbing glasses of wine, then eating hors d'oeuvres.

We all watch as Katie and Noah have their first dance, and then other couples join in.

Archer dips me, then spins me around right before kissing me. I'm not a huge fan of PDA, but right now, I want everyone to know he's mine.

"Get a room," Tyler mumbles as he dances with Gemma next to us.

"Oh, I have one. Already christened it," I blurt out, and Archer chuckles when Tyler frowns.

After we've danced ourselves silly, and the sun has long set, Katie and Noah cut the cake. The icing is a sweet hazelnut, and I shamelessly go for seconds. Right before I get a chance to chat with Katie, my phone buzzes. I almost forgot I had it stuffed in the secret pocket of my dress.

"Ms. Blackwood?"

"Speaking," I say, realizing it's my security service for the boutique.

"Just wanted to let you know the motion and smoke alarms have been tripped at your shop."

"Oh my gosh." My eyes go wide, and Archer's smile fades when he notices my mood shift. Every horrible scenario plays out in my mind.

"Are you able to go there now?" the woman asks, interrupting my thoughts.

"Yes, but I'm an hour away," I explain. My heart thuds hard in my chest.

"Alright, I'll inform the authorities you'll be there soon."

"Okay, thank you." I end the call so we can leave right away.

"What's going on?" Archer asks.

"My shop could be burning to the ground right now. We gotta leave." The happiness I felt before the call is replaced with pure panic. Archer doesn't ask questions. He just takes my hand, leading me toward the exit. We pass Tyler, and he immediately knows something's not right.

"My shop's on fire," I call out, then turn my attention to Gemma. "Let Katie know. I'm so sorry. I have to go."

"She'll understand, Ev. Keep us updated!"

Archer opens the passenger door for me, then goes around to the driver's side. He starts the engine and pulls out of the parking lot.

"How could something like this happen? Everything is up to code." I try not to cry, but my shop is my livelihood and passion.

Archer grabs my hand and kisses my knuckles as he drives us to Lawton Ridge. "I know it's really hard to think positive,

118

but it might not be as bad as you think. It could be a false alarm."

I shake my head, the tears beginning to stream. "After what I've been through this past year, I highly doubt it."

His expression falls, but he tries to comfort me in any way he can.

On the way over, I text Lexie to let her know what's going on and ask if she knows anything.

After fifteen minutes, she still hasn't texted back, and I'm convinced more than before that something bad has happened.

CHAPTER TWELVE

ARCHER

I'M TRYING my best to keep Everleigh calm, but it's nearly impossible when her shop could be in ashes. I hope that's not the case and am grateful the fire department is there. When she answered the phone, I knew something wasn't right. I've seen that expression on her face a few times and hope I never have to again.

While I drive, she logs into her security app and rewatches the last clips of video footage. I can see her growing more frustrated than she already is each time she starts them from the beginning.

"Baby, it's going to be okay," I tell her, though I have a nagging feeling that this could be linked to Krystal... "I'm here for whatever you need, okay?"

She sucks in a deep breath and finally looks at me. "I can't imagine dealing with all of this alone. I have thousands of dollars invested in my shop, and it might all be gone. And now I feel guilty as hell for not sending Katie off and rushing out without hugging her goodbye."

"Katie loves you, and she'll understand. Don't worry, she

won't be upset that you left. If anything, she's worried for you too. "

"You're right." She blows out a breath.

When we finally make it to the outskirts of Lawton Ridge, the traffic grows thicker. The main intersection is shut down, and a cop is directing traffic around the area. I roll down the window, and the smell of burning wood wafts through the air. Everleigh's tears fall more steady, but I also see the anger behind her gaze.

"Thank God," she says when her phone buzzes. "It's Lexie." Everleigh picks up the call and explains everything she knows so far. After another minute, the call ends.

"Lexie said everything seemed normal when she locked up, and she went through the closing duties and double-checked all the doors were locked."

When we're closer to the shop, I see the parking lot is full of emergency personnel. They've roped off and blocked the entrance with barricades. Luckily, I find a place to park on the street, and as soon as the car stops moving, Everleigh bolts out toward the building.

I lock the car and chase behind her.

The fire chief stops her before she can get any closer. "Hey, Everleigh."

"Chief Porter. What happened?"

"First of all, I just wanna say I'm really sorry. Looks like the fire started in the backroom. They've already got most of it contained, hopefully without too much damage."

I place my hand on the small of her back and wait with her.

"Thank you. I appreciate y'all getting here so quickly. Can't imagine what it would look like if you hadn't," she tells him. The fire department is mostly made up of local volunteers, so when something like this happens, they rush together to help.

The crackling and popping in the distance gets louder. We stand in silence, watching the flames dance.

"We're gonna need some more water," one guy says. "Afraid the embers are gonna erupt again because the wood is so dry and hot."

The blue and red flashing lights reflect off the surrounding buildings. I can't begin to describe the horror on Everleigh's face when she notices the dark smoke lingering in the front windows. She lets out a wail of a cry as I pet her hair and kiss her head.

Thankfully, they contained the fire before it spread too far, which means the structure may be fine, but the smoke damage is a major concern. Everleigh wanders over, and when she gets to the side of the shop and notices the back is still smoldering, she grows more emotional.

"You can't go back there," the fire chief tells her as several men drag the fire hose closer to the area.

Everleigh moves to a safe distance, but one with a better view. After five minutes of staring at the guys spraying water and seeing how charred the building is, she turns around. "I can't watch this anymore."

"I know, baby. I can't imagine how hard this is for you."

Everleigh narrows her eyes, then walks away and tugs me with her. That's when I see Dana standing on the sidewalk, watching the disaster unfold.

"What're you doing here?" Everleigh asks, shocked to see her.

"Oh hey. You know I live just right down the street. Wanted to see what all the commotion was about. I can't believe this, Everleigh."

Her face softens, but I can tell her guard is still up. "Me neither. It sucks more than I can even say."

While I find it odd that Dana's here, it's not out of the realm of possibilities, considering how small this town is. News travels fast, and she's not the only person out here watching. A small crowd has gathered outside.

Though I've been here for seven months now, it's not something I'm used to, and I'm not sure I ever will be. By tomorrow morning, everyone will know what happened.

Once more people arrive, the police tell people to leave, but no one listens. They're on public property, so it's their right to stand there.

After another hour, the fire is finally out, and everyone disperses.

"Show's over, folks," one of the firemen says.

A man approaches and flashes his badge, introducing himself as the detective who'll be overseeing this case. "Do you know what started the fire?" she asks.

"Without a proper investigation, I can only speculate from what we've observed so far. It looked like the back door was broken into, and the fire was started there. Typically, windows will break from the high heat, but the door was wide open, feeding the fire. Since it's past closing hours, I thought it was odd."

"That is strange. My closer said she locked up before leaving."

"You have cameras inside the shop, but do you have any in the back rooms?"

"Not where the door is shown. Just where my inventory is stored. There's a major blind spot for the security camera back there." I can see the wheels spinning in Everleigh's mind, and different scenarios flood through mine too.

"Does anyone else know that?" he asks.

Now that Natasha has been arrested, I can't think of

anyone who would want to harm her other than Krystal. The thought makes me sick to my fucking stomach. But I find it almost impossible that she'd know something like that about Everleigh's shop.

"The only people who would know that are my employees, if they were paying attention," Everleigh states.

"We'll be getting all the security footage from the company, but if you think of any other information that could help, here's my number." He hands her a business card. "And here's the case number for the incident report. You'll need to give it to your insurance company. If we find out anything else, I'll reach out to you." Everleigh gives him her number, and we thank him before he leaves.

When we walk toward the car, Officer Proctor stops us. I've seen this man too many times in the past year, and after tonight, I hope to never run into him again. When I do, it's not for good reasons.

"You've not had the best luck lately." He frowns, holding his keys in his hands.

She lets out an exhausted laugh. "I know. It seems like every two or three months, something dramatic happens. First, I get stabbed. Then I nearly get run over by Natasha. And now my shop gets broken into and goes up in flames. What else could possibly happen?"

He offers a kind smile. "That is a lot. Hopefully, things will start lookin' up for you."

"It better," she says, groaning.

Once we're back in the car, she leans her head against the seat and closes her eyes. "This is a fucking nightmare."

"Baby, I'm so sorry." It's all I can offer, wishing I could fix it all and make everything better for her.

We drive home and talk about going back to the B&B

tomorrow to get our bags. I tell her I'll call them and let them know we had to suddenly leave.

Once we're home, Everleigh crashes on the couch and buries her face in her hands. She's still wearing her bridesmaid dress, a reminder of how the night started on a high note but ended in disaster.

I sit next to her.

"Who would do this?" she mutters. "And why?"

"Krystal. She's crazy enough to want to destroy everything in my life along with the people I love," I say, feeling guilty as hell that she's been dragged into my past.

"I don't think she'd know about the camera's blind spot, though." She lets out a frustrated sigh. "I knew I needed more back there but just haven't done it because I trust my employees. I didn't even think about someone breaking in. I'm so stupid!"

"Sweetheart, no, you're not. This isn't your fault. I promise we'll get to the bottom of it and figure out who did it. Maybe we should ask surrounding businesses if their cameras captured anything suspicious. And if it *is* Krystal...then we'll have proof."

"That's a good idea," she says, but she still looks defeated.

"We'll figure it all out together, baby."

She meets my eyes and forces a smile. "I know, but it's just a lot to process and deal with. My to-do list just grew five miles long, and I have inventory arriving at the end of this week. The timing couldn't be any worse."

"When is the timing ever right?"

She sucks in a deep breath. "Never. This year has sucked for me."

Her words are like a knife to my heart. I know she's not

directing her anger at me, but it seems these problems of hers didn't happen until I arrived.

Everleigh's business is her life, and anyone who paid attention for longer than a minute would know that. Seeing her like this is heartbreaking, and maybe that's what Krystal was trying to accomplish in the first place.

The next morning, I wake up and cook breakfast before driving back to the B&B for our bags. She tossed and turned all night, and right now, we're both mentally and physically exhausted.

Before we went to bed, I sent Tyler a text and let him know what had happened. Everleigh texted the girls and gave them an update, then apologized again for having to leave early. Of course Katie wasn't upset and was more sad to learn about what happened. Relief temporarily covered Everleigh's face, but it was short-lived. No one could make her feel better, not even me.

"Biscuits and gravy with a side of crispy bacon," I present, setting a plate in front of her at the table along with her sugary coffee. Today, she looks like she's ready to kick someone's ass.

"Thank you," she says. "You made a true Southern breakfast. I'm proud of you."

"I watched a YouTube video," I admit with a shrug. "That's homemade milk gravy, not any of that packaged stuff."

A small smile plays on her lips. "Color me impressed."

While we dig in, I try to keep the conversation moving, but I can tell she's not in the mood for small talk.

"When I get back, want me to stay home with you today?" I ask.

"No, it's okay. You should go in to work. I have errands to run anyway. I gotta meet with my insurance agent, and then I was gonna call the detective to see if I'm allowed to go to the shop yet. I want to see the damage and write down what I need to do to clean it up. That'll probably take me all day, and I don't want you to cancel with your clients again over my problems."

"You're more important than them, baby."

"I know. I'd just feel guilty if you did."

Not wanting to push her, I nod. "Well, if you change your mind, just call me, okay? I'll cancel anything if you need me. Period."

She smiles. "Thank you. I appreciate that. I don't know what I'd do without you. I'd probably be going more crazy than I already am."

I reach my hand across the table, and when she grabs it, I bring her knuckles to my lips. "I'll always be here for you."

Her phone buzzes with a call, and I continue eating as she chats. Once she hangs up, she sets her cell down. "Cathy. My insurance lady. She wants to meet me to take pictures around eight thirty."

"Gives you some more time to finish your coffee."

"Mmm. You made it perfect, too."

Everleigh finishes eating, then takes Sassy outside as I rinse the dishes. When she returns, she wraps her arms around my waist and squeezes. "I'm sorry if I'm not my usual happy self."

I turn around so I can see her beautiful face. "Sweetheart, you don't have to pretend that everything is okay around me. I know it's not."

"Thanks," she tells me, and I press my lips to hers.

"You're welcome, sweetheart. I know it's a lot to deal with right now, but they say the comeback is always stronger than the setback."

"Good because I don't think I can deal with any more bullshit right now," she groans. "My life has had enough *excitement* in the past six months to last me a lifetime. But there's been some good that's happened too. Mainly meeting you."

"Glad I could be your sunshine on a cloudy day."

She smirks. "Me too."

"Want me to drop you off on my way out?" I offer since the shop isn't that far from the agency. I know they'll probably walk over there once the paperwork is done.

"Sure, I'll finish getting ready."

I fill my to-go mug full of coffee as I wait, and ten minutes later, we head out.

"Hope you have a good day, baby. Text or call if you need me. I'll be back in a couple of hours," I tell her when I drop her off. "Love you."

She leans in for a quick kiss. "Love you too."

Krystal will pay for playing this dirty little game, and I'll do whatever it takes to make sure she's caught. Everleigh doesn't deserve any of this, and it destroys me that she's being targeted, but nothing will stop me from proving Krystal's responsible.

CHAPTER THIRTEEN

EVERLEIGH

Since my shop was purposely set on fire a week ago, my life has been a clusterfuck. It took days before I was able to go inside and see the damage with my own eyes. All the video recordings from the company were sent to the police even though it doesn't show who broke in. I've watched the footage several times, hoping that I'd see or catch something or someone, but whoever it is stayed in the shadows.

Once all the evidence has been collected for the investigation, I'm finally allowed to enter the building. I salvage everything I can before the renovation company arrives to clean up the rest. While I'd been inside a few times, I couldn't stay for long periods because it was too upsetting.

I've asked my employees to come in today so we can go through some more things together. It's their first time back since I closed. Before they arrive, I pick up donuts and a gallon box of to-go coffee. I put on my respirator mask before going inside, then open the front doors. They arrive right on time.

"Hey, boss," Lexie says with Heidi and Dana next to her, and I say hello to everyone.

"So what's the plan today?" Heidi asks, grabbing a Boston cream.

"I was thinking we'd pull clothes racks out and set them up in the parking lot. An *Everything Must Go* sale."

Heidi takes a big bite. "Are you marking everything down?"

I nod. "Yep, as soon as we have everything set up, I'll post on Instagram and Facebook. I'll add a disclaimer that the items will need to be washed before they wear them, but I believe most of the stuff in the front is still in good condition. But I need you guys to wear these respirators when you go inside."

Dana stands quietly to the side, not saying much of anything.

We put on our masks and get to work. Thankfully, the weather is absolutely perfect with no chance of rain.

After a few hours, the restoration company arrives with a huge dumpster and unloads it in the parking lot behind the shop.

"Wow," one of the women says, looking in the back room. "There's nothing left but ash. I'm so sorry."

"Thank you. It's been hard to deal with, but now that you're here, maybe we'll be able to get it lookin' new again."

"We'll do our best." She smiles.

I watch as they start shoveling rubble into garbage bags before tossing them out. It's progress, at least, but it makes me sad as hell. I've put so much time, sweat, and money into my shop, and now it feels like I'm starting over again.

I was stupid to think everything would go back to normal after Natasha because whoever did this may be an even bigger monster than her. I've been wondering if Krystal is somehow behind them in an attempt to get back at Archer, but I don't know how she'd manage to get in and out without being seen on my cameras.

When lunchtime rolls around, I order pizza for the girls and me. We take a quick break and eat.

"Do you know how long it's going to take them to remodel?" Heidi asks.

"Not sure. They said it could be as quick as a month or as long as six."

"Damn," Lexie adds. "That's way too long."

"I know," I say, sighing. "But I've requested to choose my own contractor, and my agent said they'd need quotes. So, I'm gonna beg Noah to submit a bid for the job even though he's booked solid."

"That'd be amazing," Lexie says.

"And he'd bust ass for you," Heidi adds.

Dana stays quiet, and we all notice.

"What's up with you?" Lexie finally asks her when the pizza box is empty.

"Sorry, nothing. Just got a lot on my mind at the moment." She forces a smile. "You know how it can be."

"Oh yeah, I get that," I reply, but the conversation ends there. If she wanted us to know what she was going through, she'd tell us.

Another hour passes, and the parking lot is full of clothing racks. Though they smell like smoke, the discount I'm offering makes up for how many times they'll have to wash the fabric.

"Are y'all ready for the crowd?" I posted the announcement on Instagram and Facebook, then sent out a quick newsletter too.

"Yep, bring it on!" Lexie cheers.

Within five minutes, my loyal customers show up and begin grabbing things.

I have my cash register app on my phone, so we set up a small table at the front of the building so they can use their credit cards.

"I'm sorry, I don't have any bags," I tell Mrs. Ferguson, who has a huge pile of clothes in her arms.

"Don't worry, hon. I'm gonna put these in the wash as soon as I get home and start wearing them tomorrow. Just don't tell my husband. The less he knows, the better," she says with a wink, and I chuckle.

"Okay, your total is five hundred and seventy-three dollars. You saved fifty percent!"

"Wow, amazing! So I guess if he does notice, I'll tell him it was a deal I couldn't refuse." She smirks, handing over her credit card.

"Thank you, I really appreciate your support," I say, and she hugs me before leaving. There's a line of people who have as much as she did. By the time the sun sets, nearly everything is gone. I'm virtually in tears because of how many people showed up.

Heidi gives me a hug when she notices my emotions bubbling over. "See, everyone wants to see you succeed. Out with the old and in with the new."

I nod, wiping my cheeks. "Thank you all so much for helping me. Please, if there's anything you want that's left, take it."

I look at the parking lot, and the racks are almost bare, but Lexie and Heidi take me up on my offer. However, Dana doesn't.

"Well, I better get going, y'all. When will the new schedule be posted?" she asks.

Internally, I want to wave my arm around my store and remind her that it's not even operational, but I don't want to take my frustrations out on her, so I swallow the anger down. "I don't know yet, but I'll be in touch when I do," I tell her, and she awkwardly leaves. The tension is thick between us, but I have no idea why.

Lexie and Heidi pack the items they picked out in their cars, then come back over.

"Want help putting the racks back inside?" Lexie asks.

"Sure, we can store them in the front for now," I say.

Lexie and Heidi help me clean up, then we hug goodbye. Though I'm sad as hell about seeing my shop nearly empty, I head home with a smile on my face that so many people came out and purchased stuff. I was worried that everything would be a total loss, and I wouldn't be able to recoup my inventory costs, but my customers came through. Though I often talk shit about small-town drama, there are times when I wouldn't want to live or run my business anywhere else. Today was one of those days.

It's been two weeks since the renovations started at the shop, and I'm thrilled with the progress. Noah's company was hired, and he promised to go as quickly as possible.

Being able to support Noah's business is one silver lining

I've found from this. I know he's a hard worker and always gives the best quality, so it's a win-win.

Each morning, Archer and I bang each other's brains out, then eat breakfast together. He goes to work, and I stay home since I'm selling my new inventory on social media. I'm storing it all in my bedroom so I can still bring in some income, but when the boutique is open again, I'll move everything there. I haven't had as much time to focus on online sales until now, and Lexie has been my right-hand woman through it all. Once we transition to the boutique, I'll probably need to hire someone to keep up with it.

I walk into the living room and see Archer happily playing a game of tug-of-war with Sassy.

"Hot damn," he says when he eyes me up and down. "Are you a firework display?"

I snort because the Fourth of July one-liners don't get any cheesier than that. "Am I?" I prompt.

"Yeah, baby, you just made my heart explode."

My head falls back with laughter. "Really workin' on those dad jokes these days, aren't ya?"

"I try. Are we taking Sassy with us today?"

"Nah. She hates fireworks and big crowds."

"Of course," he mutters, then pulls me into his arms and brushes his soft lips against mine.

"We should probably get going," I tell him, moaning as he slides his tongue inside.

He pouts, biting on my lower lip. "I guess you're right. I know what will happen if we keep going."

I smirk. "We wouldn't make it to the Fourth of July celebration."

We both chuckle, knowing it's the truth. After Archer takes Sassy out one more time, we make our way downtown.

"You should have a huge grand reopening when you know the date and make a big deal out of it," Archer suggests.

"You're absolutely right! I had planned a Christmas in July sale for this month, but since that won't happen anymore, a grand reopening sounds even better. Send out flyers, get a huge sign for the front of the shop, hire a local band and get food trucks to come out like when Tyler opened the gym."

"I bet it'd do really well."

"Speaking of, do you want to see Noah's progress?" I ask, and he nods.

I enter, then disable the security alarm. The walls have been freshly painted, and the wooden floor was refinished. The counter is now more of a U-shape, and he even magically made the dressing rooms bigger.

Archer's eyes go wide. "Wow. It looks like it's almost done, baby."

"I know. Noah's been busting his ass for me. Put a lot of guys on it. I kinda like it better than the original. I'm so excited to reopen."

He pulls me closer and brushes loose strands of hair from my face. "Sounds like something positive did come out of this after all."

I squeeze him hard. "I guess so. It's still stressful, but as you've said, the comeback will be better."

He kisses me, and I sink into him, getting lost for a moment.

"Okay, come look at my back room," I say, leading the way. Right now, it's just a wooden structure with studs and no insulation yet.

"Do you have more space here too?"

"Noah hooked me up by bringing it out a few feet on each side."

"I would say so." Archer looks around. "I can't wait to see it when it's done."

"I also asked him to install better lighting because it was always so dark."

Archer smiles. "Baby, I'm so happy for you."

"Thanks, babe. You seriously kept me from jumping over the edge when things felt too overwhelming."

"And now it's over halfway done. Before long, you'll get back to normal, and we can put this all behind us."

My heart pounds hard in my chest, and we meet each other's eyes. "Still, I hope we can find out who's responsible. I'm not sure I'll feel completely safe until we do."

Archer pulls me into his chest and kisses my forehead. "I know, love. I know."

After I lock up, we meet everyone in the park. There's a stage set up and booths with activities for the kids. Owen runs over with a huge corn dog in his hand. There's mustard squirted up and down the sides of it in a zigzagged mess. That thing is dangerous.

"Hey, you sharin'?" I ask, pretending to steal it.

He nearly shoves it in my face. "Sure, take a bite!"

"No, no," I say with a laugh. "I was just kiddin', but thank you. Such a little sweetheart.."

"Did you get some napkins?" Katie asks him as her parents trail him with the twins in a double baby stroller. They're wearing matching outfits and hats with red and white striped sunglasses. They look adorable.

"Uhh..." Owen shrugs and takes a big bite. He already has yellow smeared on his cheeks.

Katie's mother hands him a napkin. "Thanks, Grandma."

"I brought you guys a blanket," Tyler says, pointing at a

spot that they saved for us. Archer sits, and I settle down on his lap.

"Did you really want a corn dog?" he asks.

"Yes." I waggle my brows, and he chuckles at my insinuation. "I actually think I want some chili cheese curly fries."

"That does sound good," he admits.

"I got this." I kiss him, then stand. "I'll be right back."

It doesn't take long for me to find the food stand. They're curling whole potatoes right out front, and everyone in line watches in amazement. Minutes later, I have two large plates of fries, and my mouth waters as I carry them back to Archer.

When I return, we sit next to each other and listen to the first band play some old country tunes. I eat and sing to the music, knowing all the words. Laughter and chatter surround us, and there's no doubt this is my definition of summer.

"Oh you're a Southern-Southerner, aren't you? Didn't know you knew Johnny Cash and Willie Nelson."

"Willie is my homie." I chuckle as I finish my food.

Archer throws our plates in the trash, then lies down. I lay my head on his stomach and chat with Katie and Gemma.

"How are things moving along with the rebuild?" Gemma asks.

"Well, thanks to Noah, I think it'll be finished even quicker than I anticipated."

Katie beams. "That's my man."

Noah grins sheepishly. "I'm just happy you trusted me enough to do the job."

"Of course! You're the only person who I knew would do it right," I tell him.

"Yeah, it's been an experience."

Archer chuckles.

I tilt my chin up to meet his eyes, then poke his side. Archer squirms, and everyone laughs at him.

"No, no, no," he pleads, trying to escape.

"Take it back," I offer with a wink.

He grins. "Okay, fine. Erase what I said from your memory."

"I mean, he's not lying." Tyler shrugs.

I scowl at him. "Excuse me, but I'm a ten out of ten. I'm highly recommended and give *amazing* experiences."

"I can agree with that. Would return for the exceptional service alone." Archer mocks, settling back onto the blanket, so I can lean into him.

"So, are you two…boyfriend and girlfriend?" Owen blurts out, and I nearly forgot he was within hearing range. Oops.

I meet Archer's eyes and smile. "Yep. We are."

Owen beams as I take a sip of the beer Noah brought. "Are you gonna get married?"

"Maybe one day," Archer answers truthfully. "Just depends."

"On what?" Owen asks.

"You're treatin' them like they're on trial, son," Katie interrupts with a laugh, and I can tell Owen still had more questions.

He shrugs. "Dad, can I go play with my friends?"

"Sure, but stay where your mom and I can see you," Noah reminds him.

Seconds later, Owen runs off and meets a group of kids his age.

"Is that his girlfriend?" Gemma asks, squinting her eyes, and I laugh when I see Owen hugging a girl.

"Yeah, that's Amelia." Katie sighs.

"He's going to be driving soon, ya know," I remind them both.

She groans. "I know. Lord help us all."

After the first band finishes their set, another one comes on stage and plays more modern songs.

"Do any of you want an ice cream cone?" I ask when Archer and I decide to get some, but they all shake their heads.

We take the opportunity to walk around and see how they transformed the city square for the festival. There are mini American flags waving in the ground along the parade route. Several booths have summer-themed jewelry and wreaths. I interlock my fingers with Archer's and love being open about our relationship. It's still surreal to me even after all this time.

We browse around for an hour, then find the ice cream stand that's selling butterscotch hand-dipped cones. It's so hot outside that by the time we get them, we have to hurry and eat them before they melt.

Once we're done walking around, we go back to our friends and wait for the big fireworks display. The sun won't set for a few more hours.

I'm so relaxed on the blanket, I could fall asleep. But as soon as the band starts a slow song, Archer asks me to dance. People and blankets are spread around, but I don't care and stand with him. He wraps his arms around me, then tucks his hands in my back pockets, firmly gripping my ass.

"This is perfect," Archer whispers in my ear. "I love being with you like this."

"I do too," I admit, never wanting this moment to end.

Later on, Jerry and Belinda come over with Scarlett, who's wearing the cutest little T-shirt that reads *My Daddy Fought for My Freedom*.

"Oh my gosh. That tee is adorable."

Tyler beams as he pulls her into his arms. "My sweet girl. Did you have fun?"

Scarlett sucks her fist, drooling all down her arm. I take that as a yes.

The sun finally sets, and there's not an empty patch of grass as everyone anticipates the show. Glittery fireworks fill the sky, and I can't help but look over at Archer. I inhale his scent, and he meets my eyes before brushing his lips against mine.

It goes on for at least thirty minutes, and I soak up this moment with him and our friends. At the beginning of this year, I wished we could be together, and now, here we are. We've already been through a lot of struggles, but with Archer by my side, we've gotten through it.

CHAPTER FOURTEEN

ARCHER

SPENDING the Fourth of July with Everleigh and our friends was an amazing time. It was nice to forget all the drama for a few hours and watch her eyes light up during the fireworks.

Now that I've been at the gym for eight months, my client list has grown and keeps me busy during my shifts. Everleigh's been working from home, but her shop is almost finished, so she'll be able to go back soon. It's supposed to be done by the beginning of August, just in time for back-to-school shopping.

After my first training session of the day, I walk down to the coffee shop. Even though it's the end of July and hot as fuck outside, I enjoy leaving the gym and taking short breaks when I'm not booked solid. Plus now, thanks to Everleigh, I'm addicted to drinking iced coffee lately.

When I walk in, I order a cold brew. At this point, the owner expects my boring drinks, and while she no longer teases me about it, she always smirks. I know she's thinking about it.

On my way back to the gym, my phone vibrates in my

pocket. I smile, hoping it's Everleigh, but it immediately fades when I see an unknown number. Before I even read it, I know it's from Krystal. I've now blocked at least a dozen of her numbers, but she always makes a new one.

Unknown: Do you understand that I'll destroy your life and everyone else's lives that you love.

Unknown: Your girlfriend won't live to see the end of the year at this rate.

Unknown: Neither will your sister.

Unknown: Fuck you, Archer Boone. I hope when I finally end your life, you go straight to hell. Piece of shit.

At the end of her slew of messages is a picture of Annie, and then another one pops up of Everleigh.

I immediately drop my cold brew and stop walking. "What the fuck?" I grind out, staring at the images.

Unknown: You can keep ignoring me, but the fun has just begun.

My adrenaline spikes, and I rush back to the gym. My next client arrives in fifteen minutes, but I really can't work in this state of mind, not when I have some calls to make.

Tyler gives me an uneasy look when I approach him. "Is everything okay?"

"I'm not sure. Can you cancel my next two appointments? I

have some last-minute business I need to take care of." I know I sound panicked, but I don't have time to wait for his answer. Immediately, I go outside and dial Annie's number. She doesn't pick up at first, and I grow more anxious, so I text Everleigh.

Archer: Hey, where are you?

Everleigh: I'm at home, getting some things boxed up to be moved in the shop.

Archer: I'm coming there now.

Everleigh: Okay, see ya in a few.

It's not out of the ordinary for me to run home and grab lunch or check on her since she's by herself all day. I try to get my mind right before I get there and redial Annie's number. Thankfully, she picks up this time.

"Where are you?" I'm relieved, but even I hear the worry in my tone.

"I'm on my lunch break at work. Why?"

"Thank God," I whisper, letting out a breath as I look around, making sure I'm not being followed.

"What's going on?"

"Did anything weird happen today? Or anything lately?"

There's a long pause, and I wait a moment before I lose my patience.

"Annie?" I snap.

"Nothing really, just been having a lot of car trouble. My brakes went out because my car is an old piece of shit, and it made for an almost dangerous situation. Thankfully Patricia, the nurse practitioner, is letting me borrow her van because she doesn't need it right now."

"What? Why didn't you mention this sooner?" I grow more frustrated with her.

"Because I can't afford to get it fixed and—"

"I would've sent you the money, Annie. You need to tell me this stuff."

She huffs. "I didn't want you to have to do that, Archer. I know you're trying to get back on your feet. I want to take care of things on my own. I appreciate you wanting to help, but I don't need you saving me when I'm in a bind. You've already done that enough for me."

I pick up my pace and round the corner that leads to my street. I suck in a deep breath, trying to calm down because just learning about her brakes going out pisses me off more than she knows. It also worries the shit outta me.

"I want you to move out of Wyoming," I firmly say. "Somewhere new."

"What? Why?" Her questions are clipped, and I know she's not happy with my tone.

"I don't know where to start." I linger for a few seconds. "I keep getting threatening texts. Blocking them doesn't do any good because as soon as I do it, another unknown number messages me."

"Archer…"

"The threats are getting worse, and I'm getting photos of Everleigh and—"

"No," she whispers.

"And of you and Sadie," I continue. "Krystal knows where you live, Annie. It's no longer safe for you to be there."

The silence draws on, and it's almost piercing. In the background, codes are being announced over the loudspeaker.

"Archer." Her voice lowers. "I can't afford to just pack up my life and leave. I'm a mom now and have to think about what leaving our home will do to Sadie. She loves her school and friends. We're settled here."

"You won't be settled if Krystal harms you or Sadie because that's where we are right now, Annie. This is fucking serious. Sadie is five. She can make new friends. You can find another job."

"I'm not going to live in fear, Archer, and you are not helping. Neither is this conversation."

I blow out a disgruntled breath. "I'm not there to protect you, and I can't be in two places at once. Knowing that Krystal has photos of you guys scares the shit out of me. You're the only family I have."

"You don't know if it's actually her or someone she hired. You can't be in two places at once, well neither can she," Annie says.

"Either way, I don't trust her intentions. She sends them with threats, and I feel like she's building this up to do something, to lash out, to hurt one or both of you. Do you understand how serious this is?"

She sighs. "Yes. I do. But I can't do anything about it. I could go to the police but tell them what, exactly? Someone took a picture of me in a public place, and now my brother is worried? I don't have evidence. I haven't been attacked. She hasn't approached us, so she's not in violation of the restraining order. Maybe you're blowing this up to be more than it is because she's playing mental warfare with you. She knows your weaknesses, and she's using them against you. These types of intimidation tactics are meant to cause paranoia. Ever thought about that?"

"It's deeper than that, Annie. You and I both know that

she's unhinged and was extremely upset when Chad died. Unless you've forgotten the smear campaign she went on? She hates that I got out of prison and has let it be known that everyone I love will pay. The woman is insane, and I wouldn't put it past her to put her threats into action. That's all I'm saying. I wouldn't be able to handle it if something happened to Sadie or you when I could've prevented it all."

"Listen…" Her voice softens. "I understand that, and I know she's mentally unstable, but I can't just be on the run for the rest of my life. I already left my hometown after you got sent away. I can't put Sadie through that without plausible cause. I'm keeping watch and always checking my surroundings, Archer. I promise. If anything else happens, I will make sure you're the first to know. Not so you can fix the problem, but so you can be aware. I didn't think the car thing was her because it's on its last leg anyway. Everything over here is fine. You need to relax and breathe, okay?"

The house comes into view, and I take the sidewalk that leads to the porch.

"I just love you guys so much and would be destroyed if she harms you. I'm struggling with wanting to be there and here at the same time."

"I know, and I hate that you feel that way. But I promise, I'm doing my best to keep us safe too. But anyway, my break is over now, so I gotta get back to work," she says.

"Alright, fine, but you know what would make me feel better?"

"What's that?"

I pause for a few seconds. "If you shared your iPhone location with me. That way, if I can't get ahold of you or if something goes wrong, I can at least see where you are."

She laughs. "Fine. I'll share it when we hang up."

"Thank you. Love you, sis."

"Love you too," she says and ends the call.

I suck in a deep breath, then walk into the house. Immediately, I hear music playing in Everleigh's room and find her carefully hanging clothes that arrived in her inventory order yesterday. I give her a kiss, and she's all smiles. I have to force myself not to show my anger, but she notices.

"Uh-oh, what happened?"

I slowly close my eyes before meeting hers, trying to compose myself so I don't sound like a paranoid maniac like when I called Annie.

"I got another text."

Everleigh shakes her head. "More threats?"

"And photos," I say, handing her the phone so she can see for herself.

"Did you forward them to the detective?"

"Not yet. I will right now," I say, attaching screenshots and sending them in an email. I sit on the edge of the bed, and Everleigh gets back to work, but I can feel her mood shift.

"I hate that bitch," she mutters. "I swear, I'm going to hunt her down myself if she doesn't stop. I'm tired of this. Right when things are lookin' up, she comes right back into the picture and ruins everything."

"I know, I'm sorry. This is my fault."

Her brows furrow. "No, it's not. You didn't ask for her to constantly harass you like this. I just hate that no one can do anything about it. It's so damn frustrating."

"I think she knows she's under my skin, but I think it irritates her even more that I don't respond. She has nothing to feed off when I ignore her, so she keeps trying, hoping I'll crack," I say.

Everleigh sets down the extra hangers she was holding,

then comes closer to me. I wrap my arms around her waist, pushing her against me.

"I love you so much," Everleigh whispers, threading her fingers through my hair. "We'll get through this together."

"I love you too, baby. I'm so worried something will happen and I won't be able to do anything about it. I know her words are just threats, but what if she actually harms one of you guys? We don't know how the fire started or who broke in, so then my mind wanders to her being the culprit. And if she is, what else is she capable of doing? What if she escalates next time? I want to protect all of you, but I can't. Maybe driving me insane with threats is what she wants. I'm just rambling at this point," I breathe out in irritation.

"Concerned and protective Archer is hot."

That makes me chuckle. "And somehow throughout all of this, you always make me laugh."

Everleigh crawls onto my lap, pushing me back on the bed. She hovers above me, grinding against me and teasing the hell out of me.

"I was thinking about something," she says with a devious smirk.

"Hmm?" I say, lifting up to capture her lips again.

"That we should get a dog."

I make a face. "We have Sassy."

"Yeah, but Sassy totally needs a brother or sister, plus it's what couples do, ya know? They get pets until they're ready to have babies."

I wrap my arms around her, kissing her again. "I'd love that."

She squeals, then rolls off me and stands. "Are you hungry?"

"Not really." I shake my head. We had breakfast less than two hours ago.

"Did you tell Annie?"

I nod, then replay the conversation.

"I don't blame her, you know," Everleigh admits. "I have an overbearing brother who gets concerned a lot too. It can be a bit much."

"But at least you know our intentions are sincere."

"Yes, I do." She flashes a sweet smile. "So what kind of dog do you want to get?"

"A Doberman," I say without having to think about it. "We need a guard dog. One that can rip heads off intruders."

She snorts. "They're big babies. Trust me. A friend of mine had one growing up, and let's just say, Sassy is more ferocious."

I chuckle. "Ours would be different."

"Yeah, right! What about a chocolate lab?"

"You said Sassy needs a friend. What about a husky?" I suggest.

"Hmm. Can we get more than one?" She blinks up at me.

"No way! We can't have three dogs. We wouldn't have enough time for that. We'll just have to take some time thinking it over since it'll be our first baby together."

Everleigh beams. "Or we could just make a *real* baby?"

I lean over and kiss her. "You're the only woman in the world I'd have kids with, but not yet."

"Alright, I can live with that." Everleigh paints her lips across mine. "Wanna practice?"

I groan, wishing we could. "I have to go back for my afternoon sessions…"

"Hmm…I think you can fit an extra one in right now." She waggles her brow, making it impossible to deny her.

"Fuck yeah, I can. But it's gonna be a quickie."

Everleigh removes my clothes, then hers, then within seconds, she's straddling my legs. We move together flawlessly and give each other exactly what we need. She always knows how to take my mind off things because right now, all I can think about is her.

CHAPTER FIFTEEN

EVERLEIGH

Ding.

I jump for the millionth time when the door chimes and a customer walks in. I can't complain because it's a sound I'll never get tired of hearing, especially now since the shop re-opened last week. I'm grateful for it, but I'm on edge. Lexie shoots me a concerned expression, but I look away and greet the woman who came in.

After helping her find some lovely tops and accessories, I ring her up. I notice the way she looks at me and immediately grow suspicious. When the store is empty, I sigh in relief.

"You doin' okay? You've been jumpy." Lexie asks, studying me.

I inhale slowly and relax my shoulders. "I've just been on edge lately. After the fire and the weird text messages Archer keeps getting, I'm feeling anxious."

"You need a break, Ev. You've been working nonstop since the grand reopening. You're stressed, and that just adds to it."

"I wish that would actually fix my issues, but I doubt it." I meet her eyes. "But maybe I'll leave early tonight since I'm off this weekend."

"Yeah, you should. Go have lots of hot kinky sex with your man. Then come back Monday and tell me all about it." She grins.

"Remind me to talk to you about boundaries during your next employee review."

"Oh shush. You love giving me *all* the juicy details." She waggles her brows.

After I restock some jewelry, I grab my bag and phone, then tell Lexie goodbye. I take out my self-defense keychain and walk to my car, then check my back seat before getting in. I hate that I'm so tense and on high alert, but I can't help it. Maybe Lexie is right. I just need a little R&R.

August weather is still hot in Alabama, but there's a nice breeze today, so I roll my window down and soak in the sun. I'm determined to relax while I'm off this weekend. After everything that's happened this summer, perhaps I need to talk to my doctor about my newfound anxiety. If Krystal would leave us alone or get caught already, I'd feel a thousand times better.

When I get home, all the lights are off, and Sassy's nowhere in sight.

"Sassy!" I call out, searching my bedroom and kitchen.
What the hell?

"Sassy girl, where are you?" I go to Archer's room and find it empty.

Oh my God, she's gone. Did someone steal her? Did I forget to bring her back in this morning? Did Archer come home early and take her for a walk?

Just as I reach for my phone, hands cover my eyes from behind, and my instincts take over. When I hear a man clear his throat, I jab my elbow into his stomach. He yelps, then I turn and hold up my pepper spray.

"Everleigh, it's just me!" Archer nearly shouts when he spots the spray.

I lower my aim as I try to catch my breath. "Jesus. You scared the shit outta me."

"Baby, I'm sorry. I thought you heard me."

I shake my head. "No, I was freaking out that I couldn't find Sassy. Where is she?"

Archer closes the space between us and holds me in place. "She's at your grandparents'. I wanted to surprise you, but you came home early. I'm still packing."

"For what?"

"A romantic weekend getaway." He smiles genuinely, rubbing his finger along my jaw. "I figured we could use some time away, just you and me."

My brows shoot up. "Really? You planned somethin'?"

"Yep, I sure did. I wanted to celebrate six months together."

"It's been that long already? Wow. I can't believe it." If the first time we slept together was when we started dating, which was after his birthday party in February, then he's right.

He leans in, bringing his lips to mine. "Best six months of my life, sweetheart. Even if you just tried to pepper spray me."

I chuckle against his mouth. "I was ready to tase your ass next."

After Archer finishes packing, he drives so I can still be surprised. The car ride is peaceful as the late evening sunshine splashes through the windows onto my skin. I try to soak in the last few weeks of summer before fall arrives.

"Where are we goin'?"

"Well…it's not too much farther."

I furrow my brows, wondering what the heck he has up his sleeve.

"I wanted us to be alone." He shrugs with a devious grin. "But don't worry, the views will be worth it."

Thirty minutes later, we arrive, and my jaw is nearly on the floorboard. "Wow, you weren't lying. What is this place?"

"According to the website, it's a magical mountain retreat with vintage charm," he says. "A private place for just the two of us. It's stocked with the groceries already, but we can drive into town too."

We get out of the car, and Archer grabs my hand. "Let's take the tour, shall we?"

The tall trees give some nice shade while Archer leads me around the outside of the cabin.

"That deck is off one of the bedrooms, then there's another in the back," he explains.

"The forest is so damn beautiful," I say in awe.

"Wait till you see the inside." Archer grins while he punches in the code. Once we're in, I gasp.

"The windows bring in so much light. It's adorable." I admire the rustic décor and hardwood floors. I glance around at the dining table, chairs, and a den next to it with a little couch. A large sectional that looks comfy as hell is in front of the fireplace. Archer watches my reaction with a satisfied grin. I wrap my arms around him and kiss his lips. "This is so sweet. Thank you for doing this."

He slides his hand down my back and squeezes my ass. "I might've had some selfish intentions."

I chuckle, feeling his cock harden between us. "To which I'm extremely grateful."

Once I've had the tour, he grabs our luggage. I'm still shocked he planned this without me knowing.

After dinner, we go to the hot tub. "I love you," I tell him as I climb onto his lap. "It's like you just knew I desperately needed this."

"I could tell you needed an escape." He brushes strands of wet hair off my cheek.

"I think it's all finally catching up to me."

"Well, then I'm glad I brought some massage oil."

"Oh so you're a masseuse now?" I arch a brow in amusement.

"Yep, your very own personal one."

I rock my body against his, feeling his erection beneath me.

"Everleigh, we're outside…"

"In the middle of nowhere," I remind him.

He grins. "Your level of naughty never ceases to amaze me."

"You should be used to it by now," I retort. "Six months of mind-blowing sex."

"As I've said before, I'm a lucky man."

I bite down on my lower lip, placing my hand over the bulge in his swim trunks. Why he put them on is beyond me. I wore my bikini with the intention of him tearing it off me.

"I think *I'm* the lucky one here."

He unties my bottoms as I help lower his shorts. I slide down on his cock and slowly ride him. Every ounce of anxiety leaves my body when he kisses me. The friction between us builds hot and fast, melting all the stress away.

When we're both sated and relaxed, we climb into bed and snuggle.

"This might be a presumptuous question only six months into our relationship, and I know we discussed getting a dog, but do you see yourself wanting children in the future?" I ask as he holds me in his arms.

"I love kids and hope it's in my cards. Before prison, I was certain I could never provide a good enough life to have a family…"

"And now?" I prompt.

Archer flashes a sweet smile. "I have hope now."

"I've seen you with Owen and the babies. No doubt you'd be a great father."

"Well, playing with someone else's kids and raising your own is a *little* different," he says.

"That's true. Right now, I get to be the cool, fun aunt. Meanwhile, their parents have to worry about college funds and their futures."

"But you want that eventually?"

I exhale and grin. "Yeah. I'd love to be a mom. I'll never neglect my kids like my mother did, but the fear of not being good enough has entered my brain a time or two."

Archer places his palm over my stomach. "I love the thought of you carrying my baby someday. I have no doubt you'd be the best mother."

"You say things like that, and I'm gonna beg you to knock me up right now."

He releases a choke-laugh and shakes his head. "Tyler just got used to us being together. Let's not give him a stroke. Or me, for that matter."

I chuckle, swinging my leg over him and sink deeper into the mattress. "Alright, fine. I like having you to myself anyway. I don't wanna share you just yet."

He grabs one of my breasts and squeezes. "Same."

The next morning, I wake up to Archer bringing me coffee and breakfast in bed. We spend most of the day lounging, walking around outside, and cooking. It's the most chill day I've had in months.

"Are you ready for Raphaël to give you the best massage you've ever had?" Archer says in a half-assed French accent.

I burst out laughing when he leads me into our room and motions for me to lay on the bed.

"*Raphaël*? Are you my porn fantasy come to life?"

"Yes, madame. At your service."

The lights are dimmed, and there's spa music playing from his phone. It smells like he sprayed some lavender mist too. There's a thick white towel on top of the covers, and after I remove my robe and lie on my back, I realize it's warm.

"Did you put this in the dryer?" I ask, impressed.

"Of course, only the best for you, chérie."

I can't contain my smile as I think about the effort Archer put into making this a relaxing experience for me. Earlier, he drew me a hot bubble bath and streamed classical music while he set up everything. I thought it was sweet, but this is beyond my expectations. No one has ever done anything like this for me.

"I'm gonna place this hot cloth over your eyes. Keep your arms by your sides at all times unless I move them," he orders. I have a feeling that's going to be harder than it sounds.

Once my eyes are covered, I try to release all the tension in my shoulders. Archer has complete control over my body, and I find satisfaction in that.

Archer slathers lotion between his palms. I anticipate the coldness once he touches me, but it doesn't come. He must've warmed up the bottle beforehand. His calloused hands roam over my thighs, and the rough texture feels incredible against my skin. Archer digs his thumb and fingers into my muscles, carefully massaging his way down my leg.

"Madame, you feel tense. We need to loosen you up," he states softly. I smile at his attempt at a French accent but secretly love it.

"Yes, please. Loosen me all the way up, sir."

Archer rubs my feet next, thoroughly massaging between each toe and digging into my heels. My feet are usually sore from standing all day.

After he glides his palms up, he spreads my legs apart, slowly and torturously moving his fingers to my pussy. I wait with anticipation as he teases the flesh around my clit. I inhale sharply and keep my arms still like he instructed, but if he continues to play with me, I won't think twice about grabbing his hand and moving it right where I need it.

"You're tight here too, l'amoureux," he says as he dips a finger inside.

"Mm-hmm." I moan.

"Wet too."

"Yes," I whisper.

Archer returns to my clit, rubbing lazy circles around it.

The slow motion drives me insane, and I arch my hips, begging for more pressure.

"No moving, madame," he reminds me, and I release a groan.

He swipes his fingers through my wetness, flicking and circling, slowly building me up before he stops. I grind my teeth in frustration, but he doesn't take pity on me. Archer slides his hands up my stomach, leaving me aroused and unsatisfied.

After brushing his fingertips over my chest, he gets more lotion and thoroughly massages each breast. I pray he never stops touching me.

"Are you cold?" he asks in a teasing tone after pinching a hard nipple.

"Not exactly…" I jerk my hips again, and he stifles a laugh.

His hands roam over my shoulders and neck, softly covering every inch of me. I love that he's taking his time, but right now, I want him to fuck me senseless.

"Alright, mon amour. Flip onto your stomach," he demands.

Once I'm repositioned, he picks up body oil instead of lotion. The warmth drips onto my back, then his touch returns.

"Mmm…I like that." I release a sigh when he kneads my tense muscles.

Archer takes my pleasure very seriously, focusing on every inch of my body. He squeezes between my shoulders, working out all the knots, then takes a second to wipe off his hands. Next, he rakes his nails through my hair and up my scalp. The sensation is so tingly, I nearly fall asleep.

When my limbs feel like they're no longer attached, Archer brings his hand between my thighs. The surprise sensation nearly jolts me awake, and I release a long breath when his fingers touch my pussy again.

He flattens his palm to my lower back as his other hand returns to my clit. My wetness guides him right where I need him, and soon, he's finger-fucking me deep and slow.

Breathing heavy at the intrusion, I move my hips with him, and he speeds up. Moments later, he thrusts his thumb inside my pussy while circling over my sensitive nub with the pad of his finger.

"Oh my God." I try to gain my composure. The last thing I want is for him to stop.

"You like the massage?" he asks.

"Keep going," I order.

"Don't move those arms, and I will."

Archer's thumb pushes deeper, and I know I could come from the sensation alone. The movement has my clit grinding against the towel, pushing me closer to the edge.

"I'm so close," I tell him as he rubs more oil in his palms.

"Just wait, chérie." He moves his hand toward my ass, then pushes his thumb inside my tight hole. I gasp in shock as he slowly eases in deeper. "Relax, baby."

He squeezes my butt cheeks with his other hand as he thrusts in and out, each time going farther. I breathe out when he enters, and eventually, my body relaxes.

"That's my good girl. Trust me, l'amoureux."

"I do, *Raphaël*."

Archer adjusts himself so he can finger-fuck my pussy while he thrusts his thumb into my ass. Tingles take over my body as the strongest buildup I've ever felt rushes down my spine.

"*Holy shit, I—*"

Before I can warn him, a wave of pleasure releases, and I'm

screaming his name as I come all over his hand. Archer continues his dirty assault as I try to catch my breath.

"So beautiful," Archer mutters. "I love watching you come."

"I need you inside me, *please*," I beg.

"Sorry, madame. That's not one of our services," he says, the accent returning.

"I paid for the *deluxe* package, which I'm pretty sure you have, so…" I lick my lips as I watch him adjust his hard-on. "If you *don't* fuck me six ways to Sunday, I'll have no choice but to leave a bad review. You wouldn't want that, would you?"

"You and that smart mouth," he tsks, removing his clothes as I stare at him.

"Let me suck your cock and show you exactly what it can do."

CHAPTER SIXTEEN

ARCHER

AFTER THE STEAMY weekend getaway a couple of weekends ago, Everleigh has finally calmed down. I wanted to help her work through her stress and anxiety, and I think that mini-vacation helped.

"Your form is getting better," I tell Kyle when his session ends. "How are you feeling about your competition this weekend?"

The gym started hosting tournaments for my clients to fight in a safe and structured manner. The winner gets a free week of sessions and smoothies, plus bragging rights. It was all Tyler's idea so people would sign up to participate.

"Toby has nothing on me," he retorts in his usual cocky tone.

"I don't know. He's been very focused lately."

Kyle rolls his eyes, and I grin.

"See ya later," I tell him. I love seeing the progression of the younger guys who've been training with me since I started. Every week they come in ready to learn and advance their skills.

When I run into Tyler, I let him know I'm gonna take my break since I have an hour before my next client arrives. I head to the break room and grab the sub I packed.

As I check my phone, I see a text from an unknown number. It's the first one she's sent in a couple of weeks. When I open it, there's another photo. It's a selfie of Krystal, showing the top of her black hair, and I notice she's near a playground. Behind her, I see Annie pushing Sadie on a swing set, and I nearly drop my phone as my adrenaline rushes.

I wait for her threats to follow, but they don't come. It's perfectly clear that Annie and Sadie aren't safe.

Immediately, I check Annie's location, and it says she's near her building.

Archer: Where are you guys?

Annie: At the park across from the apartment. Why?

Fuck. Krystal's watching them right now.

Archer: I need you to take Sadie and go home. Lock the doors.

Annie: Tell me why.

Archer: Please, just listen to me.

I could tell her that Krystal was there, but I didn't want to risk Annie or Sadie getting hurt. Annie will find her and make a scene. If Krystal's as close as the picture looks, she's in violation of her restraining order, but I doubt she cares. By the time the cops arrive, she'll be gone.

Annie: Okay, fine. Sadie and I are walking home.

Archer: Text me as soon as you're inside.

For the first time since the messages started, I reply instead of blocking the number.

Archer: Don't touch them. Tell me what you want, Krystal.

Surprisingly, she responds right away.

Krystal: For you to feel the pain I went through when I lost Chad.

Archer: He hurt my sister, and I was protecting her. You can have me. Just leave them alone.

Krystal: Is that a promise?

I pinch the bridge of my nose because I don't know what else to do at this point—Krystal's unpredictable.

I think about everything that's happened, and I'm convinced she's not acting alone. She can't be in Wyoming and Alabama at the same time. Someone is keeping tabs and feeding her information.

Archer: Just tell me when and where to meet you so we can handle this face-to-face.

Moments later, she sends a Nevada address.
Then Annie confirms they're home.

Krystal: Tomorrow. Come alone or I'll immediately have my team deal with Everleigh.

Motherfucker. I need to know how many people are working with her.

Archer: I'll get there as soon as I can.

I feel sick to my stomach. Everleigh will never let me go without her or backup, but I can't risk something happening to her. She means everything to me, and because of that, I have to leave her behind.

After booking a flight, I schedule a cab to drive me to the airport. I hate doing this in secret and lying to my loved ones, but I have to finish this once and for all. If I tell Tyler, he'd try to stop me or worse, join me.

"Hey, I'm not feeling well," I tell him, glancing at Gemma, who's running the smoothie bar today. "I thought maybe I was hungry, but I just threw up my lunch."

"Shit. Maybe it's the flu?" Tyler suggests, then backs away from me. "Go home and rest. I'll cover the rest of your schedule today. Just let me know how you're doing later so I can figure something out for tomorrow if you're still not feeling well."

I nod and thank him for understanding. The walk home is quick as my mind races. Though I haven't interacted with Krystal in years, there's no doubt she's crazier than I remember. I can't underestimate her. If I'm walking into my own funeral, then so be it. Protecting the ones I love is all I care about right now.

As I pack a bag, a heavy weight rests on my chest. I need to give Everleigh a reason not to come look for me. If she knew I flew to meet Krystal, she'd worry and be on a plane. She has to believe I'm never coming back, and honestly, a part of me thinks that could be a possibility.

Sassy's at my feet as I sit at the table and write her a note.

Dear Everleigh,

I refuse to keep putting you in danger. Annie, Sadie, and you are the three most important people in my life, and every day, I fear something will happen to one of you. Staying here in Lawton Ridge puts you at risk of getting hurt. The only solution is for me to leave. Don't come looking for me. This is the best option for everyone. Never forget how much I love you. Please stay safe.

-Archer
P.S. I'm sorry.

Anger fuels through me as I fold the note and write her name on it. I set it down on the kitchen counter, then look around at the place I've called home. Best-case scenario, I outsmart Krystal and return to the woman I love. Worst case, I lose my life.

I blocked Everleigh's number, knowing that if I read her upset messages or heard her voice, I'd crack. The only reason I don't turn off my phone is so I can keep tabs on Annie. I'm not telling her where I'm going or what I'm doing, but I'll be watching her location to make sure they stay put. She probably thinks I've lost my mind, and maybe I have, but Krystal could pull some shit before I arrive in Nevada. Though she sent me pictures of Everleigh, it's obvious now that Annie was always her target.

After traveling all day, I check-in to my hotel at midnight. I'm mentally and physically exhausted. Since I landed, Tyler's called me three times, but I ignored him. While on my flight, I came up with a plan, but I can't tell Tyler, at least not yet. I have no idea if it'll work, but I'm going with my gut and trusting that it will.

CHAPTER SEVENTEEN

EVERLEIGH

THOUGH IT'S BEEN a slow day at the boutique, I've stayed busy unboxing the new fall clothes I ordered. It's almost October, which means it's time for cute furry boots, Halloween-inspired infinity scarves, and pumpkin spice-themed long-sleeved tees.

Heidi runs the front of the store while I focus on hanging and pricing everything in the back. Before I know it, I've worked straight through lunch and dinnertime.

"You need to go home," she tells me after finishing all the closing duties. "All that will be here for you tomorrow."

I sigh with a small smile. "Yeah, you're right."

When I check my phone and don't see a text from Archer, I frown. He usually sends me messages throughout the day, but sometimes, he gets really busy too.

Everleigh: Hey babe, I'm about to leave work. Want a ride home?

I wait for a response but realize it doesn't show it was delivered.

That's odd.

As I walk to my car, I call him, but it goes straight to voicemail.

His phone must've died.

I don't see him walking as I drive home, so he might've already made it there.

Sassy greets me at the door, and I call out for Archer. No response. I let Sassy outside, then notice a folded sheet of paper with my name written on the outside.

I read every word on the page with disbelief. There's no way he just left.

I try his cell again. Voicemail.

What the fuck? Something's wrong.

I call Tyler, and as soon as he answers, I ask if he knows where Archer is.

"He left around lunch because he wasn't feeling well."

"Did he say he was going somewhere?" I ask.

"I assumed he was heading home to rest. Why?"

My heart beats faster in my chest, and I swallow hard. "Because he's not here. He left a note saying that he wouldn't keep putting my life at risk and for me not to go looking for him."

"*Seriously?*" Tyler snaps. "Did something else happen?"

"Not that I know of. I just don't understand why he wouldn't talk to me first. How could he just leave me like this?"

After a beat of silence, Tyler responds, "Maybe it's for the best, Ev. If his past is following him, that could ultimately affect you. He's protecting you."

"That's not good enough for me. We need to find him, Tyler. I don't care what he thinks. We're better together, not apart."

"Archer's a big boy. He can handle himself. If he left to keep you safe, then you need to stay put. We don't know what's going on, so let him handle it."

I shake my head, hot tears spilling down my cheeks at the realization that Tyler won't help me. "I can't just sit here and do nothing," I say through a sob. "I love him."

"I know, and he loves you too. But it's obvious he's dealing with something, and maybe he can't do that with you around."

"He could get hurt," I say. "What if I never see him again?"

"I don't know, Everleigh. I can try to call him, but I doubt he'll answer, especially if he didn't wait to tell you goodbye."

"He sent me straight to voicemail," I confirm. "Let me know if you hear from him, please?"

"Of course."

When we hang up moments later, I re-read his letter. I hold on to each word trying to make sense of it, but I can't.

At least when most relationships are over, the healing process can start, and there's closure. But this feels different, almost like he was being forced.

After I let Sassy back in, I go into Archer's room and lie down. It looks exactly as it did this morning. Bed unmade as usual, a lonely sock on the floor, and one of his dresser drawers half-open. Even the panties he ripped off last night are still in place. Wherever he went, he packed without disturbing anything.

Maybe that means he'll be back? I remain hopeful, but in the meantime, my heart's shattering.

How the hell were we just talking about getting a dog together to him abandoning me?

I fall asleep with Sassy next to me and wake up a couple of

hours later. The doorbell rings, and my shoulders tense. Months later, and I still hate answering it.

Looking out the peephole, I see my best friends with a couple of bags in their hands.

"It's us, Ev. Open up," Gemma shouts.

I open the door, and they're wearing sad expressions. Tyler must've said something to Gemma.

"We brought reinforcements," Katie says as she walks past me.

"And the men are watching the kids tonight," Gemma adds, wrapping her arms around me. "Let's get some food and alcohol in you, then we'll chat."

Katie offers me a glass of wine, and I take it. When I sit on the couch with Gemma, I ask her if Archer acted unusually this morning.

"No, I only saw him for a moment. He stays busy with clients, and I'm usually jumping between reception and the smoothie bar."

"Has he gotten any more threatening texts?" Katie asks.

"Well, to my knowledge, there were some sent a few weeks ago. He promised to tell me when he got them but didn't mention anything recent to me," I explain with an edge in my tone. We made a deal to be honest with each other, and he wasn't. Now, I'm pissed.

"I know you don't want to hear this, babe, but maybe Tyler's right. If Krystal is after him, it affects you," Gemma states. "As messed up as it is, he probably left without warning because he knew you'd talk him into staying."

"Maybe Krystal gave him an ultimatum," Katie offers.

"Like what? Because every scenario I think of doesn't end well for him. That's why I want to look for him. She could hurt him."

"I'm sure Archer has it under control," Gemma says.

I take a sip of my wine, glaring at her over the rim. I know she's trying to comfort me, but it's not working. The more I think about it all, the more agitated I become.

"Archer can defend himself," Katie agrees. "And who knows, he could arrive tomorrow and tell you he took care of it."

"As in…" Gemma makes a throat-cutting motion.

"No!" Katie nudges her arm. "Like she went to jail or something."

I can only hope. But something in my gut tells me otherwise, and I won't be able to sleep until Archer's back in my arms.

CHAPTER EIGHTEEN

ARCHER

THERE'S a chill in the air of my hotel room as I get dressed. Every muscle is tense, and I won't be able to relax until this is over. I couldn't sleep, knowing how badly I hurt Everleigh. This morning, Tyler sent me a few messages, and I still haven't responded. I'll explain everything to him when the time's right.

I text Krystal to find out what time I need to meet her.

Krystal: Come in two hours. And don't forget, ALONE.

Archer: I'll be there.

I get myself ready, go over the plan, then head out of the hotel.

Krystal may think she can say or do whatever she wants to me, but I'm not going down without a fight. I can't continue to let her control my life.

"Well, well, well…you showed up. I thought you'd be a

coward." Krystal is smug as hell as she stands on the porch of an abandoned cabin. Her dark hair is messy as I peer into her sunken eyes. By the look of her veiny, bruised arms, I know she's still using.

We're standing fifty feet apart. "Well, now that I'm here, what do you want?"

Her mouth curls up in an evil grin. Before she can say another word, the front door of the cabin opens, and another woman steps out.

What the fuck?

"I think you've met my roommate, Dana."

My eyes move to the woman who works for Everleigh and has been close enough to touch me. She must be the one who's been keeping tabs on us for God knows how long. But why would Dana betray Everleigh like this? How did she meet Krystal?

"The look on your face. Priceless." Krystal laughs.

I take a few steps forward. "I showed up like you wanted. I need to know that this ends right here, right now. The stalking and harassing of Annie and Everleigh stop. You leave them alone. I'm the one you want, and I'm here."

"Hmm…" Krystal paces as if she's contemplating her answer, but her arrogant smirk says it all. "I don't like to make promises I can't keep."

"That was the deal," I remind her.

"Yeah, well, seeing Everleigh's expression when her shop was on fire and you flying to visit Annie when you realized I was a threat brought me so much joy. You must've been going crazy keeping tabs on them, and it was amusing to watch. I'm not sure I want to give that up yet. However…" She pauses briefly and whips out a gun from the back of her jeans. "It's going to be so satisfying watching the life leave your eyes. It's something I've imagined for the past five years, and now I can hardly contain my excitement."

"Was that your plan all along? Fuck with the people I love to mess with me, then kill us all? You think that'll bring back your abusive druggie brother?" I snap.

Krystal glowers at me as she grinds her teeth. I can see her anger boiling, and I know I'm playing with fire, but I want to hear the truth.

"Nah, just you, killer. Messing with them was just a bonus. You reacted just how I'd hoped. Scared and fearful for the ones you loved." She releases another laugh as Dana stands close like she's her personal bodyguard. "But I knew it couldn't last forever, and I'd eventually get you alone. And look, here we are."

"I think the police would be interested in hearing about your plan, especially since you just admitted to stalking and threatening our lives. And doesn't Annie have a restraining order against you?"

"I never came within a hundred feet of her," she retorts. "Sadie, on the other hand…"

Talking about my niece in her taunting voice has my blood boiling hotter. I take a few steps closer, ready to tackle them both to the ground.

"Don't worry about the cops. Every number I used is untraceable, and you're a felon. I'll claim self-defense…by your standards, that's what we call murder, right?"

"*Interesting…*" I say just as my backup steps out of the shadows.

"Who the fuck is that?" Krystal aims her gun at him, and Dana whips out one as well. "I told you to come *alone!*"

"Well, you brought a guest. I figured it was only proper etiquette that I brought someone too."

"Very funny. Who the fuck are you?" she sneers.

"My name's Liam Evans. I'm a bounty hunter, but I'm here on a personal job." He looks over at me and winks as he continues recording the scene with his body cam. The shoulder holster he's wearing has two loaded guns, which the girls definitely notice.

"Put down your weapons," Krystal demands, growing hysterical. "Or I'll shoot."

"I wouldn't do that if I were you." I unbutton my shirt and reveal the wire taped to my chest. "Put yours down, or Liam will shoot you."

"You're bluffing. That's a fake wire."

On cue, sirens blast from behind me, and I flash her a mischievous smirk.

"You have two options here, Krystal. Lower your gun, or the police will force you to. You can either go to jail for stalking or sit in state prison for attempted murder."

Dana does what I say, and I can tell she's not as invested as Krystal is. She stumbles away from Krystal like she's in shock and is going to pass out.

"Or my third option…" Krystal loads a round and aims her gun directly at me. "I shoot you and deal with the consequences later."

"Then I'll immediately take you down," Liam confirms, drawing both weapons. "Hope you aren't accustomed to your kneecaps because my aim is on point. Don't worry, though, I'll make sure you survive. I wouldn't want you missing out on the luxuries of cell living. Oh, and I'll happily claim self-defense since you had your gun drawn first."

"Krystal, put it down," Dana whispers as the sirens grow louder.

Liam steps closer, keeping his eyes on them both. "This isn't going to end well if you don't cooperate."

I back up slowly as Liam approaches, standing between Krystal and me. Tires crunch against the gravel road, and I know we'll be surrounded by the police within minutes. "Fuck you both!" Krystal screams, then pulls the trigger.

The deafening sound of the shot rings out, and the scene plays in slow motion.

Dana screams as Liam goes down. I rush toward him as Krystal runs off. Cops swarm the area with their handguns pointed. So much happens at once.

"Dude, you okay?" I ask Liam as I scan over his body for the wound.

"Shit, I hate when that happens," he mutters, then grins.

"What?" I ask in disbelief.

Liam lifts his shirt and reveals a bulletproof vest.

"You asshole, why didn't you tell me?"

"After a couple of close calls, I learned to keep one nearby. Figured it wouldn't hurt to put it on. Glad I was right."

"Jesus Christ, I want to kick your ass." I scrub a hand through my hair as sweat drips down my face.

Grabbing his hand, I help him to his feet. "I like to keep things interesting. Thankfully, she didn't shoot you, though."

"No shit!" I tell him, noticing Dana's in handcuffs. A couple of officers have already captured Krystal, and they're nearly dragging her to the car as she spits curse words left and right.

She glares at me as she passes. "This isn't over, Boone!"

"You have the right to remain silent…so shut the fuck up," one officer says, shaking his head.

"You can't talk to me like that!" Krystal shouts in disbelief.

I can't contain my laughter. This played out better than I

imagined, and honestly, I'm shocked as hell, but happy this is finally over.

"I still have no clue how you pulled this off," I tell Liam. "Never in a million years did I think this would work. I was holding out hope but preparing for the worst."

"Nah, man. I've worked with these guys for years. It's a I scratch their backs, and they scratch mine kind of situation. Call us co-dependent."

"Yeah, you owe us one, Evans!" one of them shouts. "This was my goddamn day off!"

Liam chuckles in amusement. "Get over it, Huddy. Not like your stripper wife is waiting around for ya. She's too busy entertaining the firemen."

"That's because she makes more money than him," another guy chimes in, and a bunch of them laugh.

"Fuck you," Huddy spits out, looking their way. "Let's get these girls booked so I can go home, okay?"

"I'm gonna need a full recap of how you managed this," I tell Liam as we jump in the truck. "And a copy of that recording. Otherwise, Everleigh's never gonna believe this."

We go to the police station to provide the evidence with our statements. With the reports I filed in Lawton Ridge and the recordings from tonight, there's enough to charge her.

"In the event she gets out on bail before the hearing, I'd suggest filing a temporary restraining order. That way, if she's stupid enough to come near you again, she'll get thrown back into jail," Detective Gains explains.

"Definitely do that," Liam interjects. "I've had a few guys come for me after bailing out. Not fun times."

I'll do whatever they suggest just to be safe. "The judge may have you return to testify, but you'll be kept in the loop." I shake the detective's hand and thank him for helping.

"Sure thing. Liam's been an integral part of us putting dozens of criminals back behind bars. It's always nice when we can return the favor," he states.

"Stop kissing his ass!" Huddy blurts out from his desk.

I enjoy hearing them give each other shit, but I hold back my laughter.

Gains hands over his card and says he'll be in touch. Although this won't be over until Krystal's locked away permanently, I'll sleep better knowing she'll finally get what she deserves. No more threatening texts or creepy pictures of my sister and niece, and no more fucking with the woman I love.

"I should call Everleigh and Tyler, and tell them where I am so they don't worry," I tell Liam as he drives me back to the hotel. "I don't know who I should be more concerned about— Tyler or Everleigh. I think they're both gonna want to kill me."

"Guess I should tell ya then. Tyler called me this morning and asked if I'd heard from you. I didn't wanna lie, so I told him the truth. Let him know what we planned and that you'd call once it was over."

Shit.

"I can't imagine he was happy." I groan.

"Actually, he was. Said he had a suspicion you called me and wanted to make sure you were okay," he explains.

"Wow. I'm glad he gave me your number. Couldn't have done this without you."

"No, you couldn't have." Liam laughs. "But it was fun."

I choke-snort at his casual tone. "You and I have two totally different definitions of fun."

He shrugs, then parks in front of the lobby entrance. "Probably. My wife won't be happy to know I got shot, but she knew the risks of my job before she married me."

"Well, tell her thanks for letting me borrow you," I muse, getting out of his truck. "And seriously, thank you. I'd say I owe ya one, but after watching how you work, I'm a bit hesitant."

Liam chuckles. "Don't worry, man. A friend of Tyler's is a friend of mine, and that earns you a freebie."

We say goodbye, then I walk inside the hotel. I'm ready to fly home and hold Everleigh. That's if she ever lets me get close after leaving her. I had to make sure that if I died, she knew how much I loved her and why I had to go.

A part of me is glad that Tyler checked up on me and knows where I am. Hopefully, that means he's eased Everleigh's mind so she doesn't worry as much. I pull out my phone and type a quick text. I'll call Annie in the morning to give her the news since it's already late.

Archer: I'm safe. I'll be home tomorrow.

I hit send, then scan the key card to my room.

Before I can flick on the lights, a body nearly tackles me.

CHAPTER NINETEEN

EVERLEIGH

I HAVEN'T BEEN able to close my eyes for more than twenty minutes at a time. Every time I do, I see Archer. I called and texted him all night with no response. My heart hurts so damn much. The mixed emotions have made me sick to my stomach.

"You need to eat, sweetie," Gemma tells me as I stay slumped on the couch with a piercing headache. I've barely moved since she and Katie left last night. "I brought you some food from the deli."

"I'm not hungry," I mutter as I stare at the wall.

"Try to eat it anyway," she demands. "Tyler's on his way over right now."

I blink up at her. "Why? Did he hear from Archer?"

"Not sure. He just said he was coming."

I swallow hard at the possibility of Tyler knowing something. As soon as he walks in, I jump to my feet.

"Where is he?"

"Everleigh, relax please."

"Tell me!" I snap. "If you know something, you can't keep that from me."

"He's in Nevada with Liam."

"What?" Gemma and I both gasp.

"How does he know Liam?" I ask.

"I gave Archer his number a while back. I told him if he was ever in any trouble that he could call him for help, so I guess he did."

"What happened? Did Krystal do something?" I ask.

"I don't know much, Ev. But it did have something to do with Krystal. I called Liam this morning, and that's all he said. Promised he'd have Archer let me know when it was over."

I narrow my eyes. "When *what* was over?"

He shrugs. "Liam didn't say."

I pace the living room. "Why wouldn't Archer tell *me*? Or bring me with him? I could've helped!"

"Krystal was threatening you and Annie to get to him. Honestly, I'm glad he chose to leave, or I would've had to step in," Tyler states.

"What?" I ask, shocked. "How could you say that?"

"Because your life was in danger. Regardless of our friendship, you're my sister, and I'll always protect you."

"I'm a grown-ass woman. I can defend myself. And that's no excuse for him bailing on me. We could've done this together." Tears surface again, but I don't care. I could've lost Archer forever, and I'm pissed that he kept me out of the loop.

"He made his choice, Ev. You need to sit here and wait because this is the safest place for you right now. If I hear anything else, I'll tell you, okay?" he says in his soft big brotherly tone. It irritates me even more.

"I think he's right, babe," Gemma chimes in. "Plus, Liam is the best at his job. Whatever they're doing, Liam won't half-ass it."

I only know Liam through Tyler, so I don't have a personal

relationship with him, but he better make sure Archer returns in one piece.

Once I've settled back on the couch, we chat for a few more minutes before they leave for work. I glance at Sassy, and she gives me those sad puppy dog eyes as if she's wondering where Archer is too.

"I can't just sit here and *wait*," I mutter to myself, reaching for my phone and searching for Maddie's number.

Tyler met Liam in California years ago. When Liam started dating Maddie, my brother immediately knew we'd get along, so he gave her my number. We started casually talking, which led to phone calls and FaceTimes until, at some point, we were chatting weekly. After a while, we both got busy with life, but we still keep in touch. If anyone has information on Liam and Archer's whereabouts, it's her.

"Everleigh! Hey!" she answers.

"Where's your husband?" I immediately ask, not in the mood for small talk.

"Uh, why?"

"Because he's with my boyfriend, and no one can give me any info as to where he is."

"Archer didn't tell you where he was going?"

I sigh because I know how that sounds. "No, and you're my last resort."

"I booked two hotel rooms in Vegas, but that's all I know, sweetie. Liam told me about a crazy chick they were gonna get arrested but didn't say anything else."

Shit.

"Can you tell me which hotel?"

"Sure, let me screenshot and text you the confirmation email."

"Great, thank you."

"Everything okay?" she asks after I receive the image she sent.

"I don't know, but is there any chance you can call and add me to Archer's reservation?" I beg. "I can explain everything later, but for now, I need to get on a plane and make sure he's okay."

"Yeah, babe. I got you. I'll do it right after we hang up."

"Thank you."

After the call ends, she sends me a message confirming she took care of it. I managed to book a flight for this afternoon, which means I need to pack and haul ass to the airport.

After I have everything I need, I drive Sassy to my grandparents', giving them only a couple of details. Once I'm on the highway, I speed and make it just in time to board my flight. I breathe a sigh of relief when I'm in the air, soaring toward the man I love.

When I finally see him again, I'm going to squeeze him tight enough to break his ribs, then smack him for leaving me. I'll make sure he's okay first, then be mad.

I take an Uber to the hotel once I land. Luckily, it's off the Strip, so I don't have to deal with thousands of tourists. If the circumstances were different, I'd be excited to be in Vegas.

Once I arrive and get a speech about their amenities, the receptionist hands me the room key and directs me to the elevator.

"Thanks so much."

I wheel my luggage to the elevator and head up to the sixteenth floor. I knock before entering so I don't scare him, but no one answers, so I let myself in.

The room is dark, so I flick on a light. His bag is on the floor, and the bed is unmade. I didn't think about what I'd do once I arrived, so I make myself comfortable and hope he returns soon.

I decide to freshen up in the bathroom, then realize my phone is still on airplane mode. As soon as I turn it off, I'm flooded with voicemails and texts from Tyler and Gemma.

Tyler: Mimi said you dropped off Sassy hours ago. Where the hell are you?

Gemma: Babe, send me your location. I'm getting worried.

Tyler: I swear to God. Answer me!

Since Gemma was nicer, I respond to her first.

Everleigh: I flew to Vegas, just got to Archer's hotel room.

Instead of responding, she immediately FaceTimes me. Tyler's scowling next to her.

"I told you to stay put!" he scolds.

"I couldn't…"

"Ev, I thought something happened to you. Could've given me a heads-up," he says.

I shrug. "Well, I knew you'd try to stop me."

"Sounds eerily similar to what Archer did to you," Tyler says, and I shake my head.

"It's different, trust me," I say.

Gemma speaks up. "So is Archer there?"

"No, but his stuff is, though."

"How'd you even know where he was staying?" Tyler asks.

"I called Maddie."

He rolls his eyes. "Of course you did. She'll be gettin' a nice little chat from me later."

"You realize I'm thirty-four years old, right? Not a child. A fully grown woman."

"After all the shit I've seen and been through over the years, I don't care if you're eighty-fucking-five. If I tell you not to get involved in trouble, you should listen."

"Whoops." I shrug.

Gemma smirks, clearly trying not to take sides. "When're you flying home?"

"I didn't plan that far in advance. Only booked a one-way ticket."

"Keep me updated," Tyler says just as his phone goes off. "Wait, he just texted me."

"What'd he say?" I shout.

"I'm safe. I'll be home tomorrow," Tyler reads, and there's a collective sigh.

"Thank God," Gemma says.

"So where is he?" I ask.

"Probably with Liam," Tyler responds. "I'll text him and find out."

"Alright, lemme know."

We say our goodbyes, and I pace the bathroom as my mind reels. It's actually spacious, and the lighting is great.

As soon as the door creaks open, I race out and leap into his arms.

"Holy fuck!" Archer yelps as he catches me. I hang onto him as tight as I can as if he might disappear. "Everleigh?"

"I'm so goddamn pissed at you," I murmur with tears falling. I'm so damn relieved to see him.

"Baby, what're you doing here?" He walks in farther, then

sits down on the bed with me on his lap. "I can't believe you're here."

I meet his concerned eyes. "I was a mess. How could you just leave a note? Do you have any idea how scared I was?"

"Sweetheart, I'm so sorry." He slides the pads of his thumbs over my cheeks. "I had to make sure you'd be safe. If I had told you my plan, you would've never let me face Krystal."

"Damn right," I scold. "I had to track down Maddie just to find out where you were. No one knew anything."

"It all happened so fast. I called Liam before I left, and he agreed to meet me here. He had a whole team of cops ready to back us up. He's seriously badass."

"So I've heard," I say. Tyler shared a ton of stories, and Maddie mentioned the trouble he'd gotten into over the years.

Archer cups my face and presses his lips to mine. "I'm not happy you traveled alone, but I'm selfishly glad to see you."

"You should know I'll never accept you walking away from me, got it? Your protectiveness has nothing over how possessive I am of you."

He flashes a crooked amused grin. "I'll do whatever it takes to make it up to you."

"Yes, you will," I confirm. "But first, you need to tell me everything."

Archer and I end up in the tub as he starts from the beginning. Even I'm amazed by how effortlessly Liam's plan worked out, though I shouldn't be too shocked. He's a pro and doesn't take shit from anyone.

"That fuckin' bitch, Dana. I knew I should've fired her," I seethe when he mentions her involvement. "My gut feeling told me something was off with her. The secret roommate. Her being there when the fire happened. She took pictures and kept tabs on me for that psycho. I hope they give her a harsh sentence."

"Yep, you were right," he says calmly as he rubs a washcloth over my back. "The detective said Dana was cooperating and wanted to make a plea deal. With her confession and testimony, Krystal will hopefully get prison time."

"And what's gonna happen to Dana?" I ask.

"Not sure, but if they charge her as an accessory, she'll go to jail for sure."

I didn't necessarily hate Dana. In fact, I tried to be the best boss I could and even her friend. While I wasn't perfect at that, I only wanted the best for her. It's going to take me some time to heal from her betrayal. What did Krystal offer her that would convince her to turn against me?

Hopefully, I'll get to ask her those questions one day.

Once we're out of the water and dried off, Archer holds me under the covers like he does every night. I can't imagine not spending the rest of my life with this man.

"So, you really wanna make it up to me?" I taunt.

He arches one brow. "What'd you have in mind?"

CHAPTER TWENTY

ARCHER

I WAKE up with Everleigh's legs intertwined with mine. After she arrived the night before last, we decided to stay a couple more days to explore. We spent yesterday doing tourist things and shopping.

Then we celebrated all night long.

"Mornin', hubby," she murmurs with a sleepy grin.

I smile wide at the sound of that. "Good morning, my beautiful wife."

Everleigh giggles. "Wow, that sounds so…"

"Weird?"

"I was gonna say amazing, but sure, let's go with weird."

I chuckle, bringing her mouth to mine. "Weird. Amazing. Unbelievable. Surreal."

"All of the above." She moans against my lips. "Everyone's gonna freak out when they hear."

"Do you think Tyler's gonna kill me?" I ask.

She shrugs. "Should we FaceTime them and see?"

"Sure, might as well do it before we go home."

It takes Everleigh ten minutes to find clothes and freshen up.

"Good to go?"

"Yep!" She grabs her phone and calls Gemma.

"Oh my God, finally!" Gemma's face fills the screen.

"Hi!" Everleigh greets. "Where's my brother?"

"Right here." I hear his moody voice in the background, then soon, he's next to Gemma.

"Cheer up, bro. We have some exciting news!" Everleigh's bursting at the seams with happiness, and I love this look on her.

"You're pregnant?" Gemma squeals.

Everleigh furrows her brows. "No!" Then she holds up her left hand and shows off her ring. "We eloped!"

"What?" Gemma screams at the same time Tyler yells, "You what?"

I wrap my arm around Everleigh and smile. "Guess that means we're officially family now," I tell Tyler, hoping he won't lay me out for this.

"How in the hell did that happen? I mean, congrats! But oh my God, I didn't see that comin'," Gemma says, her mouth still open in shock.

"To be fair, I only suggested we *look* at rings. Ya know, give him a little hint, show him what I like. I didn't expect him to get down on one knee and propose! Right there in the middle of the jewelry store." She looks over at me and beams. "How could I not say *yes*?"

"But whose idea was it to get hitched in Vegas?" Tyler asks.

"It was a mutual decision. We were walking around and saw a chapel. Then looked at each other and said…why the hell not?"

"Uh…because you've known each other for less than a year?" Tyler interjects.

Gemma elbows him in the side.

"Excuse me, big bro. You eloped without telling a soul, making us believe Gemma actually married Robert! You two don't get to say a damn word," Everleigh remarks with a shit-eating grin. "You guys kept it a secret!"

"We had to! But that's beside the point. Does this mean we'll finally get a niece or nephew now?" Gemma lifts her brows, waiting for an answer.

"Let us enjoy being married for a bit, okay?" I interject.

"We've got time," Everleigh adds. "Though according to my period app, my biological clock is ticking."

Gemma giggles.

"Aside from you someday knocking up my sister, Archer, I'm happy for you two. My stance still stands, though." He gives me a pointed look.

I break her heart, he breaks my skull. Got it.

"I knew you were adventurous," Gemma tells Everleigh, then glances at me. "But I didn't know *you* were such a risk-taker, Archer."

"There's no risk when you're marrying the woman of your dreams. Only anticipation for what your future holds."

"Aww…." Gemma says.

"You're too sweet, baby." Everleigh leans in and kisses me. "And I agree. We've survived a lot together and have gone through more shit than most couples ever do. So, why waste time when you want the same things?"

"That's true. Plus, when you know, you know," I add. "I didn't think twice about putting that ring on your finger."

"Jesus, you two." Tyler grunts. "You're gonna be attached at the hips now, aren't ya?"

Gemma smirks. "They already are. I'm so happy for you two. Seriously. I can't wait to celebrate with y'all."

"Speaking of, when are you coming home?" Tyler asks. "Mimi's ready to send Sassy to the shelter if she eats one more shoe."

Sassy has separation anxiety because even though she's a little shit sometimes, she's never chewed on our shoes before.

"Tomorrow. That okay, *Dad*?" Everleigh rolls her eyes. "We want one more honeymoon night."

"We'll eventually go on a real one," I tell her confidently. She deserves more than just a couple of nights in a hotel room in Vegas.

"Well, text me your flight times," Tyler says. "Your clients are waiting."

"I'll be back at work the day after tomorrow," I confirm. "Appreciate you taking them on."

"Yeah, you're welcome. Some of them have real foul mouths, though."

I laugh. "Don't I know it."

We say our goodbyes, then Everleigh tosses her phone. "Everyone will know before our plane even lands."

"That's small-town living for ya." I flash her a wink. "And good, I want everyone to know you're *mine* forever. My wife. The future mother of my children. The love of my life."

"You're gonna get me pregnant with all this sexy talk," she taunts. "But first, we better call Annie."

"Alright, but let's make it quick. I need to get back inside you."

My cock is hard as fuck, and I want nothing more than to devour my wife, but she's right. After I explained the whole situation to Annie yesterday, she nearly lost her mind. Annie was pissed I put myself in harm's way and didn't tell her what was going on. Of course I apologized profusely, but since it all worked out, she couldn't stay mad for long.

I click on Annie's number, and when she picks up, Everleigh holds up her hand.

"Holy shit, what's that?" she exclaims.

"Bad word!" Sadie calls out, and we both laugh.

"Say hello to your new sister!" Everleigh grins.

Annie's eyes widen as she brings the screen closer. "No freaking way! You two got married?"

"Yep, we sure did," I confirm.

"Are you telling me my only brother didn't invite me to his wedding! I don't know if I should be congratulating you or mad." She pouts.

"Uncle Archer!" Sadie comes over. "Hi, Everleigh!"

"Hey, sweetie," I say.

"So are you my aunt now?"

"Uh, yeah, I guess so!" Everleigh smiles.

"Yay! Can we come visit soon?" Sadie asks, and Annie takes back the phone.

"So why did you two decide to suddenly tie the knot?" she asks.

We repeat what we told Tyler and Gemma. By the time we finish explaining, Annie's shoulders relax, and she says how happy she is for us. I apologize for not telling her sooner.

"We'll make plans for y'all to visit real soon, okay?" Everleigh says. "Now that everything has calmed down, you have to come."

"Well, give me a heads-up, so I can request off work," Annie says. "And book flights."

Everleigh looks at me with a cheeky grin. "How about six weeks from now?"

"Six weeks?" Annie gasps.

"Yeah, the middle to end of October is the best time to come to Lawton Ridge. There's even a huge fall festival with tons of trick-or-treating. Y'all would love it!"

"Yes! I wanna go! Mom, can we?" Sadie begs.

"I'll do my best, okay? See if my boss lets me take some vacation days."

We chat for a couple of minutes, then finally I tell Annie I need my wife. She gags, then hangs up.

"*Finally*." I toss her phone on the floor.

"Hey! I need to call Katie and my grandparents too." Everleigh squeals, but I pin her to the mattress and grind my hips against her. "Never mind. They can wait. Fuck me right now."

I flash her a devilish smirk. "Hold on tight, Mrs. Boone."

Lowering between her thighs, I slide her shirt up her body. I press a kiss to her lower stomach where her scar is. It's not huge, but it's a reminder of what she went through and how strong she is. Next, I move up between her breasts and roll my tongue over her nipple. She releases a soft breath and arches her back.

"Your tits are so sexy, baby." I move to the other one and suck. "Your little whimpers and moans drive me crazy."

"You know what would be really crazy?" she asks.

I feather kisses down her stomach as my hands cover her breasts. She breathes heavily as I pinch her nipples.

"Hmm, tell me," I say when she doesn't speak.

"You fucking me against the window and showing all of Vegas what's yours."

I look into her eyes. "Excuse me?"

"Too much?" She bites down on her lower lip, looking innocent.

"You wanna be on display, baby? Tease every man who sees you? Let them look at something they'll never touch?"

"God, yes." She pants. "Show off your wife."

"Jesus Christ, Everleigh." I get to my feet and drag her out of bed. "I'm so goddamn hard."

She waggles her brows, leading me to the floor-to-ceiling windows. "Give me your best, hubby."

Everleigh rests her palms against the glass as my nerves take over. I've never had public sex before, and I have never let anyone watch. But it's different with her. It always has been, and I love the spontaneity in our relationship. Everleigh's an adventurous person, and I like that she brings that out in me.

Luckily, the sun's shining, so unless someone's focused on the hotel windows, they won't be able to see much. However, I love that she likes the idea of someone watching us. Makes it more sexy.

I move behind her, giving her ass a hard smack. She yelps, then looks over her shoulder with a mischievous grin. "You ready?"

Fisting my shaft, I stroke it a few times and tease it down her crack. "Can't wait for you to squirt all over that window, baby."

Everleigh arches her back, then spreads her legs, giving me a full view of her pussy.

"Look at that pretty wet cunt." I growl, pushing against her until I'm inside.

"Mmm, yes," she hums as I ease in deeper, her tight walls already squeezing me like a vise grip.

"Keep your hands on the window and spread your thighs," I murmur in her ear as I fill her to the hilt. "Let Vegas see your perky pink nipples as I fuck this perfect little pussy."

"Oh my God," she groans as her head falls back. "That feels amazing. Don't stop."

I tightly grip her hip with one hand while wrapping the other around her throat. She rocks against me, meeting me thrust for thrust, as she struggles to catch her breath. Loud moans fill the room as she pleads for more, demanding I let her come, but I don't allow it yet.

As my rhythm slows, I slide my hand down and slowly rub her clit. "You're so close, sweet girl. Your body's fucking begging for it, isn't it? You wanna come all over me."

"Please, Archer. God, it's agonizing. I'm almost there…" she pleads, grinding her body into mine.

"I wonder how many are enjoying the view right now," I whisper as I brush my lips along her neck. "How many people in the other hotels are getting a free show? How many people on the street can see your juices dripping down your legs? I bet they wish they were me," I taunt, then suck on her skin. "I wanna mark you everywhere. Put my baby inside you and let them know you're mine."

"I'm yours," she murmurs, pushing against the window to get more friction. "No one could ever love me the way you do."

"Goddamn right," I say with pride, slapping her swollen clit.

Everleigh yelps, then with one hard thrust, she's screaming out my name. As her body shakes, she struggles to stay on her feet. I cage her against the glass as I slide out, and she gushes like a volcano that hasn't erupted in a million years.

"Jesus fucking Christ," I hiss when she bends over and flashes me her pink lips. "You're soaked."

Everleigh faces me, then moves over a few inches. "Lift me up."

"What?" I ask, stepping closer.

She wraps her arms around my neck, then jumps. I quickly catch her and cup her ass cheeks. "Against the window," she orders.

I smirk. "What a bossy little wife I have."

"Ooh, that glass is cold." She shivers when I press her back to it.

"It won't be for long," I promise, then feed my cock into her delicious pussy.

I keep one arm underneath her and the other planted next to her. As I pound her against the glass, she squeezes her legs around my waist and tightly holds me into her. Though I've always felt close to Everleigh, this is a new experience that I'd only ever want to do with her. The love I feel for her is indescribable. Nothing compares to the feelings we share. She consumes my thoughts, and I often wonder how I'm good enough for her. Each day, she finds ways to remind me why we're perfect together.

"I love you so much," I whisper against her lips.

She hangs on to my shoulders as she twists her tongue with mine. "I love you, husband. I can't believe I get to call you that."

"Till death do us part, sweetheart."

"Fuck that. We better die at the same goddamn time because I'm not living one second without you," she admits.

I chuckle, and a warm shudder runs down my spine. "I want you to come again, babe. I'm so close."

"Tell me you want me," she says between heavy breaths. "I'm almost there. Tell me something really dirty to push me over the edge…"

"You know I want you, every fucking day, all the time. I

want you on your back with your head leaning over the bed as I throat-fuck you into oblivion."

"Archer, Oh my God…" Her eyes flutter closed as her thighs squeeze. She lets out guttural moans, letting everyone on our floor know she's having the greatest orgasm of her life.

Once she recovers, I set her down on her feet. "Okay, we're doing that throat thing right now…" she demands, leading me to the bed. "And you better come all over me too."

"Sweet Jesus, you're gonna make me explode before I even get started."

She chuckles as she goes to the bed, then lies on her back, exposing her long smooth throat for me.

"You're sure? We don't have to."

She opens her mouth wider and reaches for me. Positioning my dick, I slide between her luscious lips and immediately feel the warmth. Slowly, I glide in deeper, and when I hit the back of her throat, she chokes but stops me from pulling out.

Her taut nipples stand at full attention, and I pinch them between my fingers. When Everleigh widens her legs, I reach down and play with her greedy clit.

At this rate, we're never leaving this room.

And I'm one hundred percent on board with that.

Moments later, my balls and legs tighten.

"On your chest, baby," I tell her so she releases me. I pull out with a deep groan, pumping my come all over her tits. Her creamy skin is marked with red handprints and bite marks, and the possessive side of me loves its visual.

I fall on the bed next to her, my heart racing. Before she can move, I quickly grab a towel and clean her up.

"That was amazing," I tell her, feathering kisses along her jaw. "You're gonna be sore."

"Good. I like feeling where you've been." She waggles her brow with a devilish grin.

"You're filthy, you know that?" I shake my head with a smile. "But that's why I married you."

"So my bubbly personality and bedtime snuggles didn't seal the deal?"

"Oh, that's what drew me in, but your naughty words and top-notch blow jobs kept me."

She rolls her eyes as I toss the dirty towel. "Funny because I remember someone trying really hard not to sleep with me while simultaneously sleeping next to me."

"Hmm, yeah, I remember that too. Except in my memory, you seduced me, and I was too helpless to stop it."

"Oh please!" She swats at me, but I quickly grab her wrist and pull her up onto my lap.

"Mm-hmm, I like it when you beg."

"You think we'll ever get sick of each other?" she asks as my cock twitches against her leg.

"Not in a million years. Since the first night you slept in my arms, I wanted you close. There was never going back after that."

CHAPTER TWENTY-ONE

EVERLEIGH

I CAN'T BELIEVE it's been two months since Krystal and Dana were taken down and arrested. Last week, they were finally sentenced. Dana took a plea deal and was sentenced to two-hundred hours of community service with the requirement of staying away from me. The rumor mill chewed her up and spit her out, and she couldn't handle the glares and whispers around town.

It was very obvious she wasn't welcome at the boutique, and no one else trusted her enough to hire her. After a month of not being able to find a job, she packed up and moved. It's better that way.

On the other hand, Krystal was sentenced to eight years in prison, mainly because of Archer's documentation over the months and Dana's confession. Krystal had planned to attack Annie and Sadie after she killed Archer. I was last on her list.

I'm just so damn thankful he did what he did and that Liam was able to come through for him.

It took nearly a year, but Archer and I finally feel safe in Lawton Ridge. While I won't go anywhere without my self-defense keychain, most of my fears have vanished. I love being married to Archer, and we're excited to start planning for the future.

As I put on the breastplate to my Wonder Woman costume, my phone rings. When I see Tyler's name flash across the screen, I pick up.

"Hey. I'm almost ready. Tell Gemma to quit stressing."

He chuckles. "I wasn't calling about that."

"No? Something wrong?"

"Not really." He pauses. "I just got a call. They caught who was responsible for Eric's murder."

My breathing increases. "Oh my God. Who?"

A long sigh escapes him. "It's Mafia-related. Victoria's dad never got over her loss and somehow linked it back to Eric's involvement. The hit man was arrested for another crime and confessed."

The silence draws on, and I'm not sure what to say. I was convinced Natasha did it since she was so distraught over his affair.

Archer stands in the doorway dressed as Captain America. He sees my face and asks me if I'm okay. I nod so he doesn't worry. After the Krystal drama, we don't keep anything from each other.

Once I end the call with Tyler, I tell Archer the news.

"Wow," he says. "I guess his wife knows then?"

I shrug. "I'm sure she does. No telling what she'd have done if she hadn't been convicted."

He wraps his arms around me and holds me tight. "She was crazy, but I can't imagine the pain of losing a spouse. Even if Eric didn't talk about her or if it was arranged, she seemed to care about him a lot. Grief can make people do crazy things."

"If something happened to you, I'd act the same way," I admit as he leans forward and steals a kiss.

"Me too, babe. Don't want to even think about it. Oh, do I have lipstick on my mouth now?" he asks.

"Nah, I could literally get on my knees right now, and this stuff would still be perfect."

Archer chuckles. "That's actually kinda hot, and I'd like to test that out. Whatcha say, wifey?"

He steps back, getting a full view of my costume, and smirks.

"Hold on, I need to get my headpiece before you make a judgment." I run to the bathroom, then position it on my head. Sassy comes chasing behind me, and that's when I notice she's wearing a Thor costume. I nearly fall over laughing because it looks like she has human legs.

"Poor baby." I bend down and pet her. "What has he done to you?"

Archer meets me in the hallway. "You love it."

"Yeah, but now my Sassy is gonna steal the show!" She runs around, and I can't get over how cute she looks. The kids at the trunk or treat are going to be hysterical over this.

"Yes, she will," he says in a baby voice, then his phone vibrates. "Guess I'll have to take a rain check on the lipstick test. Sadie and Annie will be here in fifteen minutes."

They arrived last night and stayed in a hotel next to the airport. Then this morning, they checked out and will be staying with us tonight.

"Awesome!" I say. "You don't think Annie will be mad that I have an entire giant-size bag of candy for Sadie, right?"

Archer shrugs. "We can spoil our niece any way we want. There's nothing she can do about it."

I pull him into a hug. "I love that you call her our niece."

"She is, sweetheart. That ring on your finger says so."

Before we get too caught up in the moment, I pull away and take Sassy outside. Archer fills the pumpkin bucket to the brim with candy. Moments later, there's a knock on the door.

Archer grabs his shield, and we answer it together.

"Trick or treat!" Sadie says with a big grin.

"All treats!" I tell her, wrapping her in a hug. "Your costume is amazing."

"I'm Black Widow!" she squeals as they enter.

"I know, and she's a bada—" Archer elbows me before I can continue. I clear my throat. "Bad to the bone!"

"We got you something," Archer admits, handing over the plastic holder filled with full-sized chocolate bars. Sadie's eyes are as wide as saucers as she starts digging inside.

"Mommy, they're big ones!" she gasps with excitement.

Archer meets Annie's annoyed gaze. She purses her lips then smiles. "Tell Uncle Archer and Aunt Everleigh thank you."

"Thank you!" She squeezes me, then Archer, and that's when I noticed Annie is dressed like Dark Phoenix. She's wearing a bright red wig and a one-piece suit that fits her like a glove.

"Wow, you look incredible."

She laughs. "I guess I understood the superhero assignment."

"I'd say so. Gonna get some dates tonight," I tease, and she shakes her head with a smirk. Before I can say anything else, Sassy makes her big reveal.

"Aww," Sadie says, bending down to pet her. The giggles that escape Sadie as Sassy tries to lick her are adorable. "Is she coming with us?"

"Yep, she is! As long as there are no fireworks, she's good

in public. She loves kids," I say as Archer places his hand on my shoulder. I give them a quick tour of the house, and Archer helps them unload their things. He places everything in my bedroom since we're still sleeping in his room.

As we make small talk, Annie glances at the time on her phone. "Oh we should probably get going."

"Yes, yes, yes!" Sadie jumps up and down as I grab Sassy's leash.

Annie meets Archer's eyes. "And that's her level of hyperactivity *before* full-sized chocolate bars."

I chuckle. "I was kinda to blame too."

"Thankfully, someone's staying at Aunt Everleigh and Uncle Archer's tonight!" Annie sing-songs as Sadie skips outside.

We load into my car and drive to the event center. This year, all the local businesses, churches, and nonprofits got together to make the Tenth Annual Trunk or Treat bigger than ever before. The Chamber of Commerce even hired a food truck to serve free corn dogs, and there's a hay maze and pumpkin carving contest too. When we drive through the town square, I'm shocked by how many cars are parked on the street.

"I think we're gonna have to park and walk, babe," Archer says when we notice how crowded it is. Once we're out of the car, Sadie grabs Archer's hand and holds it until we get to the entrance. In the distance, I can hear a band playing spooky-themed music and smile at how amazing everything looks.

"Hey!" Tyler walks up. He's dressed like Batman, and Gemma is Catwoman. I nearly choke when I see they've dressed Scarlett like the Joker in makeup and all.

"She's going to kill y'all for this when she's older." I let out a howl of a laugh.

Gemma crosses her arms. "Just know, we played rock, paper, scissors on who got to pick her costume, and I lost. She can be mad at her father for the pictures that'll circulate at her wedding."

"Whatever. I know she's gonna look at these pics and think how freaking cool her dad is for dressing her like this!"

"It's only her second Halloween!" Gemma reminds him.

"And she'll have many more where she can choose to be whatever she wants." He lets out a chuckle as he picks Scarlett up and shows her off.

"Okay, I have to say, it is adorable," Annie speaks up. I introduce her just as Katie and Noah come over with the kids. Sassy tries to lick everyone that passes us and loves all the attention.

Owen's dressed like Thanos and is wearing a huge glove with jewels on his hand. Noah's the Hulk, but I can't quite place who Katie is. She's wearing a red leather coat and boots.

"Okay tell me," I say, pointing at her outfit. "Who are you?"

She reaches below the stroller and puts on a mask. "What about now?"

"Are you freaking Star-Lord?"

She snorts. "Yes! I wanted to match Owen and the twins."

I then noticed they're dressed as Groot and Rocket. "*Guardians of the Galaxy*. Super cute."

I look over at Noah and chuckle. "What happened?"

"I was originally supposed to be Yondu, but I had an allergic reaction to the blue paint. This is all the Halloween store had left," he explains with a shrug. "Only took thirty-something years to figure out that latex paint ain't for me. Probably not a bad thing, though. It's kinda humid. I'd probably look like Genie from *Aladdin* that you all bought off Wish with as much as I sweat."

"Wow, at least you found something last minute, geez!"

He nods. "Yeah, I looked like a creep without the paint."

Owen holds out his hand and shakes Sadie's. "Nice to meet you."

"You too," Sadie says, staring up at him like he's her new big brother.

"Okay, so tell me how this works," Annie says. "It's like a maze in here."

Gemma laughs and points. "So we start at this end, then go all the way around to the pumpkin carving and hay maze, then end at the booths."

"Oh my goodness, there's so many! Hopefully, she'll be good and tired by bedtime." Annie glances around, and I can just tell she's already having a good time.

"Probably not by the time they eat all the sugar in their bags." Katie snorts. "But I'll say a prayer for you and me both."

We wait in line for our first stop. Little ones surround us, and they're full of energy. When we finally show up to the boutique booth, Lexie beams with excitement.

"Oh my God. I have to get a picture of all of you. And Sassy! Pure freakin' cuteness." She pulls out her phone and snaps pictures like she's the paparazzi. Heidi and Sandy, my new employee, are giving out candy to the children and boutique coupons to the parents.

"Trick or treat!" Owen and Sadie say in unison to the girls.

Lexie grabs three big handfuls each and fills their bags.

"Thank you!" they exclaim, then head to the next one.

"Let me know if you need anything," I tell Heidi.

"Just a husband who will dress up with me like you and Archer," she says, lowering her voice. "Married people goals."

I lean in and whisper, "I've perfected blow jobs."

She shakes her head and snorts. "You'll have to give me your secrets later."

We snicker, then I follow the group who's already at the next one. The adults stand back as the kids walk up, and I smile at how protective we look—like real-life superheroes.

Sadie and Owen are having a great time, and a few parents stop to have their little ones take pictures with us. But of course, Sassy continues to steal the show. As we pass the pumpkin carving area, Sadie asks if we can do one, and we all agree.

"There's a contest going on right now, too," one of the teenagers says. "You just put your pumpkin up on the ledge over there to be displayed. You can pick them all up after trick-or-treating. Judging starts at six thirty."

"I'm gonna win!" Owen announces confidently.

Owen and Sadie start carving, giggling, and teasing each other. It's messy, but they're having a blast pulling out the guts with their bare hands. Once they've finished putting silly faces on their pumpkins, we help carry them to the front.

"I bet you'll win," Noah tells Owen. "That's a freakin' masterpiece."

"I dunno. Sadie's is really good," he offers, giving her a sweet compliment. Sadie gives him a toothy grin as they walk back.

"This is so incredible," Annie says. "Really giving me small-town vibes."

"Just wait till Christmas in Lawton Ridge." I wink.

"You know, this is a good place to raise a kid," Gemma tells her, and Katie agrees.

Annie glances at Archer with a smirk. "So I've heard."

"It's a great place to raise an adult too." Archer interlocks his fingers with mine.

Tyler chuckles. "I don't think I'd ever want to live anywhere else with my family."

"Same," Noah agrees.

"Mom! They gave me a toothbrush and toothpaste!" Sadie runs up to Annie.

She snickers. "It's the local dentist, sweetie."

"She was nice. Told us to brush and floss after we eat our candy!"

"Brilliant." Archer chuckles.

"She's been doing that since I was a kid," I say. "But I'm sure you're better at brushing than me."

Sadie nods as she pets Sassy on the head.

Archer leans in and whispers in my ear, "Yeah, 'cause you're my dirty girl."

A blush sweeps over my cheeks.

After we've visited every booth and eaten too many corn dogs, we go through the hay maze. It's clearly built for kids, and we can see over the hay wall, but we follow Owen and Sadie through it. They get lost a few times and fall into a fit of laughter. It takes us nearly twenty minutes to reach the end, and it's obvious that Sadie's growing tired. She and Owen got so much candy. Their bags were so full, they had to get another one. The twins and Scarlett are getting fussy, and even Owen's yawning, so we know it's time to call it a night.

"Please don't be a stranger," Gemma tells Annie as we hug and say our goodbyes.

Since we're parked a few blocks away, Archer carries Sadie to the car. She's nearly fallen asleep by the time we get there.

On the way home, Sassy lies on my lap while Archer drives us home. Even she's exhausted from all the excitement.

"Thank you so much for making this such an enjoyable evening. I had a really good time," Annie whispers.

Archer turns to meet her gaze. "What do you think? You like it here?"

Annie laughs. "I actually love it. Well, from what I've seen anyway, but I get really good vibes."

"Then I guess that means you should move! You are family, after all." I take the opportunity to remind her how much we'd love for her to be here.

She sighs. "I dunno. I'd need to find a job first."

"You're just in luck. The school nurse just retired, and they've been searching for someone with the right qualifications to replace her. Mrs. Abernathy told me in the grocery store yesterday."

A wide grin spreads across her face. "Seriously?"

"You should apply, sis. You've got a lot of experience, and you're great with kids. I bet you'd be a shoo-in," Archer says.

"I would love that." Annie sighs, and I can tell she's contemplating it.

"And hey, if that doesn't work out, I could always use another manager at the boutique."

"Really?" Annie asks. "You'd hire me?"

"Absolutely!"

"And that means I'd be closer to you two. Sadie seems to love it here too. All the kids were so nice to her tonight. Especially sweet Owen. She'd fit right in." Annie's lost in thought as we pull into the driveway. Archer slides Sadie out of the back seat and carefully carries her inside, then puts her in my room.

She speaks up when it's just the three of us hanging out in the kitchen. "Oh my God. Am I really considering moving?"

"Yep! And it's going to be great. You can even use my spare room until y'all find a place," I offer, removing the headpiece from my hair. Archer's eyes soften. It's not something we've talked about, but I know how much it'd mean for him to have Annie living here.

"Then we'll finally be able to be one big happy family," Archer says, pulling us both into a hug.

Annie and I both laugh.

"I can't wait!" I beam with excitement.

"Honestly, me either," Annie says. If Lawton Ridge can win me over in less than twelve hours, there's no doubt in my mind that it's where we're meant to be."

CHAPTER TWENTY-TWO

ARCHER

It's Everleigh's favorite time of the year, which means the house is decked out in red, green, and gold. The tree is trimmed, and my closet is full of Christmas sweaters. I can't even be mad about it because it makes my wife happy, and that's all that matters. I love seeing her eyes light up when she sees all the decorations. This year, Everleigh has even added a train set that moves on a track around the tree. Sassy loses her freaking mind every time it starts playing music, but it's kinda funny.

Since it's our first Christmas as husband and wife, I want to make it extra special, but it's going to be hard. Everleigh's extra when it comes to the holidays, but I think I figured out what will make this year stand out.

At least I hope.

Annie and Sadie just flew in, and I know Everleigh's overly excited about them being here. They're staying in our spare room until their place is ready, but the moving truck won't arrive for a few more days.

"Everleigh?" I look around the house and find her in the

bathtub. "There ya are. We're supposed to be at Jerry and Belinda's in an hour." They've invited everyone over for Christmas Eve dinner.

"Don't worry, I'll be ready. Just wanted to test out my new waterproof vibrator."

My eyes widen as I lower my eyes to the bubbling water. "What happened to BUB?"

I laugh at her cute pouty face.

"He retired. So I had to get a new one."

I step in closer. "Oh really? What's this one's name?"

"BUB 2.0. The speeds are...." She puts her fingers to her mouth and smacks her lips together in a chef's kiss.

"Not sure if I should be happy about that or not." I furrow my brows, then roll up my sleeves. "I'll be the judge of that."

"Be my guest."

I lower my hand into the warm water and slide between her thighs, where I find a bullet vibrator massaging her clit. Instead of turning it off, I move it to her nipple.

"What're you doing?" she asks, breathing faster.

"You'll see, my love." I flash her a wink, then push my finger inside her pussy.

"That's intense," she mutters as I move it to her other nipple. My thumb rolls over her clit, circling it fast and hard.

"When you need to come, you ask me. Got it?"

"Mmm...that feels so good," she hums as her eyes flutter closed and her body sinks deeper into the tub.

"Should we see how long it takes you to get there? Because we're on a time limit, baby."

"You know what I need, so do it," she demands with a cocky smirk.

Everleigh loves dirty talk. She loves hearing what I'm

going to do to her or what I want her to do to me. As soon as I start talking, her body responds.

"Your cunt is so tight. You squeeze my fingers so good," I tell her, adding a second digit and thrusting deeper. "I love when my cock's inside you and your juices spill all over me. I wanna feel you lose yourself on my fingers."

I slide the vibrator to her clit, and she releases a loud moan as I increase the speed.

"Now you're just torturing me," she whimpers, spreading her legs wider.

"Imagine if my mouth was on you. Sucking your tits and marking your skin."

"I say let's show up late for dinner," she pleads.

I chuckle in amusement as her body shakes and begs for its release. "We can't. Belinda's worked all day to cook for us."

"Fine, but just know your Christmas present is something you'll want to use tonight. It was gonna be your wedding gift, but then I figured I'd wait."

"Well, now I'm intrigued. What is it?" I ask, keeping my pace as her body trembles. It's been four months since we got married, so it's impressive she's waited that long.

"Remember that sex shop we went to in Vegas? Well, when you went to the restroom, I found some special anal lube and was gonna surprise you."

I nearly choke on my tongue.

The corner of her lips tilts up in a seductive smirk. "I want you to bend me over and spread my ass cheeks."

"Jesus Christ." I pull my fingers out of her, then slam them back inside. "You can't just spring something like that on me when I can't do anything about it."

Everleigh giggles, arching her back as I drive deeper. "It's my gift to you."

My hand stalls, and she meets my gaze. "Baby, that should be pleasurable for us both."

"I'm sure it will be once I get used to it, but you're the only person I've ever let be there. I want to go to the next level."

"You're seriously killing me here…" I adjust my cock. It's so goddamn hard it's painful.

Just when I'm contemplating doing all the sexy things with her, the bathroom door bursts open. Sadie enters with Sassy trailing behind her.

"Hi, Uncle Archer! Hi, Aunt Everleigh!" she squeals.

I've never scrambled so hard to turn off a vibrator and get to my feet, hoping I don't look suspicious. Immediately, I place my hands over my crotch to hide the very noticeable erection.

"Sadie, hi," I say awkwardly.

Everleigh moves lower into the water, hiding her breasts and BUB 2.0.

"What are you doing, kiddo?" I ask.

"Mom dropped me off because she had to run an errand quickly. She told me to let you know I was here." She flashes an innocent smile, and I want to curse my sister out right now.

"Oh, alright. Well, let's give Everleigh some privacy to finish her bath. Wanna play with Sassy outside?" I suggest.

"Yeah! C'mon, Sas!" she calls out, and the dog goes chasing after her.

"I cannot believe a five-year-old just cock blocked me," I murmur when we're finally alone again.

Everleigh holds up the bullet with a naughty grin. "Sorry to hear that. I'm gonna finish, then get dressed."

"No." I quickly swipe it from her grip, and she squeals in protest. "You don't come without me. If I'm suffering with blue balls, *so are you*."

"That's not fair! I was in here minding my own damn

business when you interrupted, and now you've stolen my orgasm." She crosses her arms over her chest and pouts. "Hand it over."

"It'll make an appearance later with the lube." I back up to the door and wave it in the air as I leave. "But for now, he's going into hiding."

"Archer Boone! Get back here!" she screams. I laugh as I hide it in the freezer. If she wants it, she'll have to deal with it freezing her clit off.

"What's Aunt Everleigh yelling for?" Sadie asks when she returns with Sassy.

"Don't worry, sweetie, she's fine. Are you excited that Santa's coming tonight?"

"Do you think he knows I'm here? I didn't get a chance to send him a letter with our new address before we moved." Her sad expression pulls at my heartstrings.

"Oh, honey, you don't have to worry about that. He knows *exactly* where you are! You're gonna wake up tomorrow and have a ton of presents under the tree," I confirm.

"Yay!" She wraps her arms around me. "Thanks, Uncle Archer."

"You're welcome, Sadie." She runs off, and Sassy follows her.

Moments later, Everleigh walks out with a towel wrapped around her body and a scowl on her face. "That was mean."

I smack her ass and wink. "It was for your own good, baby. The anticipation of getting the orgasm of a lifetime will make it that much hotter."

She rolls her eyes, then walks past me to our room. She looks at me over her shoulder and glares.

"Love you!" I say with a chuckle.

She flips me the bird, and I blow her a kiss.

We've been at Jerry and Belinda's house for a couple of hours, stuffing our faces with turkey, ham, and all the fixings. Then Belinda served three different pies. I almost asked Everleigh if she was making her Better than Sex cake, but with Annie and Sadie moving in this past week and her boutique's end of year sale, there was no time.

Owen and Sadie sit next to each other on the couch, playing the Nintendo Switches that Jerry bought them. The twin boys just turned one, and Scarlett had her first birthday a couple of months ago. All three of them are walking and into everything.

During her party, Gemma and Tyler announced they were pregnant with baby number two. Of course, everyone was excited and happy for them. I think it's great they're growing their family, and I hope one day to have that with Everleigh. Right now, she's focused on the boutique and even mentioned opening a second one in Mobile. I'll support her decision because I love seeing her chase her dreams.

I've been saving money since I started working at the gym and hope to build my credit so we can buy a bigger house in the future. Though I love where we live now, it's not big enough for what I have planned.

"So I have a little something I want to give to you," I tell Everleigh as everyone listens. "I had help getting it and figured I'd bring it out since it's here."

"Oh my gosh. Show me already!" Everleigh shrieks.

"Okay, hold on. Gotta go to the cottage."

Everleigh gives me a weird look, but I grin. I go to Gemma and Tyler's house that's behind Jerry's. A few months ago, Tyler mentioned they were looking for a bigger house because more space is needed for the new baby. As soon as they find something, Annie and Sadie will move into the cottage. Everleigh loved the idea, and I'm ecstatic they'll still be close to us.

Belinda's even more excited because she adores Sadie. She's already told Annie they're invited to dinner every night. Since Annie got hired as the elementary and middle school nurse, she'll work daytime hours and be home in the evenings. I'm so happy it worked out because she hated working those long swing shifts.

I return with a large box in my hands, and Everleigh's eyes widen when she sees me. "Holy crap, what is that?"

Before I can say anything, a little bark howl gives me away. Everleigh stands with her jaw on the floor. "No way. Is that a puppy?"

Kneeling in front of her, I set it down, then open it. She immediately bursts into tears as she stares at the puppy who's looking at her.

"You actually got me a husky puppy?" She picks him up, then holds him to her chest.

"I did, for this exact reaction, sweetheart. Merry Christmas."

She nuzzles her face against his nose. "He's so sweet. Thank you, babe."

Owen and Sadie come over and ooh and aah over him.

"What's his name?" Sadie asks.

"We still have to pick one out," I say, wrapping an arm around Everleigh and kissing her forehead.

"I'm seriously so shocked right now." Everleigh beams.

"Tyler and Gemma helped and kept him for five days."

"Scarlett's obsessed with him," Gemma says. "You better give us visitation rights."

Everleigh laughs, then sets the puppy down so the other kids can meet him.

"You should name him Chase," Tyler says. "Considering that's all you're gonna be doing."

Gemma snorts and agrees. "He has a lot of energy, that's for sure."

"I love it actually," Everleigh says, playing with him on the floor. "I can't believe you all hid this from me."

"We knew you'd lose your mind," Gemma says.

"I can't believe he's all mine. This is the best Christmas gift I could ever ask for." Everleigh's eyes soften when she meets mine.

I lean in and press my lips to hers. "I love hearing that. I hope Sassy adapts to not being the only child anymore."

She snickers. "God. Yeah right. She's a spoiled princess."

Everyone takes turns holding and playing with Chase. After an hour, we help Belinda clean up, then decide to leave so we can help Annie get ready for Santa coming.

"I think this puppy is gonna be more challenging than I expected," Everleigh says over coffee the next morning. Between taking him out and hearing him whine nonstop, we got zero sleep.

"I think a newborn would've been easier," I say around a yawn. "At least they stop crying when you pop a boob in its mouth."

She snorts.

Chase comes barreling in from playing with Sassy outside. We watch as the two wrestle and bark at each other. So much for our quiet mornings together.

I don't regret it, though.

Seeing Everleigh's face light up when she first saw him and catching them snuggling together last night is worth the sleepless nights. I know it'll get easier and we'll adjust.

"He really is so dang cute," Everleigh says as Chase sleeps on his dog bed.

"Yeah, when he's not awake," I quip.

"Uncle Archer!" Sadie shouts, and we quickly shush her, but it's too late. Chase's head pops up. "Oops, sorry."

"It's okay. What do you need, sweetie?"

"Chase was chewing on this. Should I throw it away?" she asks, coming closer with something in her hand.

"What is it?" I narrow my eyes.

She hands it over, and when I realize it's a pregnancy test, I look at Everleigh, who's as white as a ghost. I swallow hard as I read the word PREGNANT on the small screen.

"Sadie, can you give us a minute, please?" I ask, and she nods, walking back to Everleigh's bedroom.

"I guess that's my Christmas gift to you," she says softly. "I was gonna tell you tonight over a romantic dinner."

I blink hard in disbelief. "Come here."

She moves closer, and I immediately pull her onto my lap. When she wraps her arm around my shoulders, I place a palm over her stomach. "We're having a baby."

"Are you happy about that?"

I cup her face, bringing her mouth to mine, and passionately kiss her. "I don't think I've ever been more happy in my life, sweetheart. Since we weren't trying, I'm surprised but not at all disappointed."

When tears spill out, she wipes her cheeks, and I hold her tighter. "I haven't had much time to process it, but as soon as I read the test, I was beaming with excitement."

"Since this was our first Christmas as husband and wife, I wanted it to be perfect. One you'd never forget, but I think you've just made this the best one for me."

She presses her mouth to mine. "For both of us."

"I love you." I slide my tongue between her lips.

"I love you too," she murmurs.

"Do we still get to use the anal lube?" I ask, waggling my brows.

She bursts out laughing, then smacks my arm. "I'll be

surprised if we ever have sex again with Chase, the cock blocker."

"Thank God we've decided to crate train him. He'll get used to it soon and won't whine all night long. I hope." I blow out a breath.

"At least we'll be ready for those sleepless nights. That right there is our baby in training. By the time ours is here, we'll be pros."

I laugh. "That's one way to look at it."

She kisses me softly. "Don't worry, Daddy. We've got this."

I arch a brow, already loving how that sounds. "Daddy? Can you use that in bed from now on?"

"Tell me where you hid my vibrator, and I'll scream it all night long," she taunts in a seductive tone.

The corners of my lips tilt up. "He's in the freezer."

Her eyes widen in horror. "Archer! I'm not gonna be able to use it now."

I snake my arm around her waist and smack her ass. "Exactly. You made a vow to give me all your orgasms. I'm just making you keep your promise."

She narrows her eyes. "Does this mean no jerking off in the shower?"

"Haven't done that since the day I got you, baby."

"Why?"

"Because you're insatiable." I wink. "And I only wanted to experience it with you."

She shakes her head in disbelief. "You are way too damn sweet for your own good."

I brush a finger along her face, sweeping away the flyaway hairs. "Nah, only for you."

EPILOGUE
EVERLEIGH

Dear Everleigh,

I DIDN'T WRITE you a special letter on our wedding day ten years ago, so for our vow renewal, I wanted to give you something you could keep forever. Besides my heart, of course. You'll have that till death parts us. But according to you, we have to die together so neither of us has to be without the other. Well, I'm still on board. I can't imagine living a single day without your love. The highlight of my day is seeing you in the mornings with your coffee, wearing a messy top bun and baby spit-up on your shirt from the night before. I'd never be able to survive without your witty comebacks, spontaneity that gets us lost in the middle of nowhere, or hearing you scream my name into a pillow so the kids don't hear us. I lived thirty-three years before I knew the real definition of happiness, and that wasn't until I met you. You and the girls are my whole world.

So today, when I recite our vows for the second time, know that I love you on the deepest level. Thank you for falling in love with me and letting me fall for you. Every moment together has been a dream. Even when we struggled to balance work and family life, you were always by my side.

And I'll say this till the day we die—I'm a very lucky man.

I can't wait to see you in a wedding gown. I already know you'll steal my breath away, but I wanted to give you your *something blue*. Put it in and meet me down the aisle.

I love you, baby.
-Archer

I read over his last sentence. Put it *in*?

His letter left me speechless with tears surfacing, but I blink them away so I don't smear my makeup. I grab the box that the envelope was attached to and open it.

That dirty *motherfucker*.

I snicker at the blue mini bullet inside with the remote missing. He's a sneaky devil, but I can't deny him, so I lift my dress and ease it inside. Then I send him a message.

Everleigh: Just so you know, when you pull this out of my pussy, I'm using it on you tonight.

Archer: Pfft. I'd like to see you try.

Everleigh: My ass will be sitting on your face, giving you a front row seat when we 69.

Archer: Did you really have to put that image in my head as I'm about to stand next to the pastor?

A vibration soars through my body, hitting deep inside, pulsating on and off.

Jerk.

Everleigh: This is gonna be torture. There's no clit stimulator, so I'm just gonna be teetering on the edge all night.

Archer: That's the point. You'll be so wet and ready for me when I strip off your dress.

I groan at the realization that I won't be orgasming anytime soon.

"You good, Ev?" Katie pops her head into the bridal suite. "They're ready for you."

Nodding, I smile wide and grab my bouquet. Tyler meets me in the hallway, and I loop my arm through his.

"Thanks for walking me down, even though I'm in my forties." I chuckle.

"That doesn't matter. You'll always be my little sis." He grins.

We only invited close friends and family. The ceremony is short and sweet, but this time, we recite our own vows. By the time we kiss, there's not a dry eye in the place.

After Archer and I go down the aisle, we scoop up the kids and take family pictures. I still can't believe we ended up having three girls. We thought our last baby was a boy, even decorated the nursery in fire trucks and picked out a name, but we got the shock of a lifetime the day she was born. And to no surprise, she's the most unpredictable one of the three. She was exactly what we needed to complete our family.

"Well, Mrs. Boone…we have the night to ourselves. You ready to play?" Archer clicks on the remote, and my hips jerk.

"I swear to God, if you don't give me what I need, I'm shoving this up your ass."

"Tsk, tsk. Such foul language for a pretty lady." He walks behind me and reaches for the zipper.

The speed increases, and my knees threaten to buckle. He only clicked it twice throughout the party, but he's constantly tortured me since we've been alone.

Archer slowly unzips my dress, brushing his lips against my mouth. "Tell me what you want, baby."

"Something we haven't done before," I reply.

He chuckles. "Not sure that option exists."

"You sure about that?"

Archer slides the silky white material down, and I'm left in only panties. He comes around and meets my eyes. "Well, now I'm not."

"Sex tape," I blurt out, and his brows shoot up. "Too much?"

"It's never too much with you, but I didn't expect that one." He snakes his arms around my waist, pulling me into his chest. "It's exactly why I love you so much. Every day's an adventure."

"Gotta keep us young and hip," I say with a laugh.

"That's true. So, you want to record it here?" He glances around our master bedroom. "Or in the shower?"

"Let's start here, and we'll see where it goes…" I suggest in case I change my mind later and we end up somewhere else.

"Don't have to convince me." He swats my ass. "I'll set up the tripod."

The camera is aimed at the bed, though I know we often end up against the wall or loveseat next to the window.

Honestly, this room was the sole reason we bought this house. Well, besides the land for our four dogs to run free. The large suite makes for a nice sanctuary for us to spend alone time together. A huge master bathroom is attached with a shower and whirlpool tub. We've christened it hundreds of times too.

Archer adjusts the bullet to full speed while I kneel in front of him and suck him off. I love meeting his eyes and feeling empowered as the pleasure rocks through him. With the remote in his hand, he changes the speed every few seconds. He fists his fingers in my hair as I pick up and slow down my pace.

"Fuck, you're beautiful with my cock in your mouth," he growls as I pull him deeper down my throat. "You like me owning your pussy?"

I nod with pleading eyes, hoping he'll give me what I need. The buildup has been torture, and I'm ready to explode.

"Put me out of my misery," I beg, massaging his balls.

"Do what I say then," he demands, tilting up my head until our eyes meet. "Rub your clit."

I move a hand between my legs.

"Nice and slow, baby. Don't rush," he orders.

I lazily rub circles over the swollen bud while swirling my tongue around his sensitive tip. He clicks the remote and adjusts the speed, putting it on a fast, consistent vibration.

"Oh my God, yes," I murmur, trying to concentrate.

"Everleigh." His deep tone grabs my attention, and I snap my gaze back to his. "Don't come."

"I need to!"

"On my cock, only."

I release a groan, ready to beg. "Get your clit nice and ready for me. I bet your pussy's dripping wet."

"It is," I confirm. "I'm so close."

"Bend over the bed," he says, and I quickly obey.

He smacks a hand on my ass, then smoothes it with his palm. "Spread your legs. Let me see that needy cunt."

Before he's even inside me, his filthy words nearly have me unraveling. Archer knows exactly what I like, and his dirty talk is what I always crave. He can set my body on fire with just one sentence, and he knows it.

"That's my girl." He strokes himself a couple of times before pushing inside. I gasp at the intense sensation, then rock my body into his as we move in sync.

Archer leans over me and covers my hands with his as he impales me with deep, hard thrusts.

"My beautiful wife, squirting all over me as I fuck her. God, I'm a lucky man," he mutters in my ear.

"Shit, that's so good. Don't stop," I whimper, meeting him movement for movement.

After he slides a hand between my legs, Archer pinches my needy clit, setting me off. My walls tighten and squeeze him as liquid gushes down my thighs. Archer groans in my neck, slamming into me a few more times before he releases inside me.

As I collapse on top of the bed, he falls next to me. "You have three minutes to rest. Then I'm hauling your ass against that window." He winks, reminding me of our wedding weekend in Vegas.

Archer keeps every promise he makes. By the time the sunrise beams through the blinds, my legs are numb, and I can barely walk. I feel him on every inch of my skin, and now, thanks to our naughty video, it's a night neither of us will *ever* forget. Though even without it, I would've replayed this night for the rest of my life.

"Mornin', my love." Archer brushes his lips over my jawline. "Breakfast?"

"Yes, please," I say. "The girls will be home soon."

"Guess you better refuel then so we can make our shower documentary."

I burst out laughing. "Rain check, I'm too sore for a double feature."

"Alright, fine." He presses his lips to mine. "Stay in bed. I'll bring up your coffee and food."

Once he's gone, I check my phone and let Annie know she can bring the kids when she's ready. She and her husband were nice and offered to take them for the night. Of course, Sadie offered to help babysit too, and at fifteen, she's proven to be very responsible. When Annie and Smith got pregnant four years ago, Sadie really stepped into her big sister role. She and Owen are still best friends, but he's in his third year of college at the University of Alabama on a baseball scholarship, and since Sadie's still in high school, she only sees him when he's home for breaks. Gemma and I both think they're going to end up together in the future, but only time will tell.

However, if they don't, Annie's son and Gemma's youngest daughter are the same age. Tyler and Gemma had a boy when Scarlett was two, then got the surprise of a lifetime when they found out they were expecting again. Now their oldest is eleven, and it's safe to say they're staying busy with three kids while running their businesses.

"Here you are," Archer says, carrying in a tray of food.

"Mmm...smells delicious." I lower my eyes down his body. "The view's pretty decent too."

"You keep teasing me like that, and I'm telling Annie to keep the kids another night."

I chuckle, taking a sip of coffee. "I think she's going a

little crazy." Considering she moved into our old two-bedroom house after we bought this one, they're definitely crowded. Sadie didn't mind sharing with her baby brother at first, but now he's getting into everything, and she wants her privacy. When my three go and stay, they usually end up having a slumber party in the living room. But I know she and Smith are looking for a bigger place now.

"It's a really good thing you're snipped, or last night would've definitely done the job a fourth time," I say, eyeing his low-hanging boxers.

"I could get it reversed, and we could try for a boy." He winks, climbing on the bed.

"Oh my God, get off me with that talk." I playfully swat at him. I love our children more than anything, but after my second shop opened in Mobile last year, I'm already stretched too thin. Luckily, Archer's been a big help with juggling duties and working less at the gym. Smith happily took the extra hours.

"Oh come on, Scarlett will be old enough to babysit in a couple of years, and then we just pawn our kids off on her."

I laugh at his "solution" and tell him no way. Scarlett, Finn, and Luke are eleven and little hormonal pre-teens. A phase I'm definitely not looking forward to with our own. It's a miracle Katie and Noah haven't lost their minds yet dealing with double trouble.

Archer and I lay in bed, eating and enjoying our coffees in peace. It'll be short-lived, but we're taking advantage of every minute alone.

"Did you enjoy yesterday?' he asks when we're finished.

"Yes, of course. Didn't you?"

"Absolutely. Best second wedding I've ever had." He

smirks, then rolls on top of me. "Thanks for marrying me ten years ago and again yesterday."

"Thanks for askin' me." I lean up and kiss him. "It's wild to think about everything we've been through the past ten years."

"Yeah, especially considering how far we've come."

"And I couldn't imagine doing it with anyone else."

"Hell no, baby. You've always been the one."

"When did you know I was?" I ask curiously.

"That first day we met. Something inside me shifted, and my heart knew."

I furrow my brows and slant my head. "The day after my birthday when you found a naked man on my couch?"

"Yep." He nods. "I mean, I wanted to punch the guy in the face, but I loved how you carried yourself with that no fucks given attitude. I knew right then you'd be a good match for me and were someone who could handle all the demons I was facing."

"As much as I love hearing that, I'm glad you left that story out of our vows." I chuckle, just imagining Tyler's reaction, considering how pissed he was at me that day.

"Our story will always be my favorite. It's been a wild journey," Archer says sweetly.

I snuggle into his chest as his arm wraps around me. "The best kind there is."

"Couldn't agree more."

And they all lived happily ever after till death parted them.

If you haven't started at the beginning of the Lawton Ridge duet series, make sure to catch up with Tyler & Gemma's duet with *Keeping You Away* and Noah & Katie's duet with *Pushing You Away.*

WANT MORE?

If you enjoyed the Lawton Ridge duet series, make sure to check out the Bishop Brothers and Circle B Ranch series. They're filled with hot Southern men, big family drama, and small town antics.

If you haven't met Tyler's bounty hunter friend, Liam Evans, who helped take down Krystal, then check out the Roommate duet series. These are filled with slow burn romances that grip your heart with every word!

ABOUT THE AUTHOR

Brooke Cumberland and Lyra Parish are a duo of romance authors under the *USA Today* pseudonym, Kennedy Fox. Their characters will make you blush and your heart melt. Cowboys in tight jeans are their kryptonite. They always guarantee a happily ever after!

CONNECT WITH US

Find us on our website:
kennedyfoxbooks.com

Subscribe to our newsletter:
kennedyfoxbooks.com/newsletter

facebook.com/kennedyfoxbooks

twitter.com/kennedyfoxbooks

instagram.com/kennedyfoxduo

amazon.com/author/kennedyfoxbooks

goodreads.com/kennedyfox

bookbub.com/authors/kennedy-fox

BOOKS BY KENNEDY FOX

DUET SERIES (BEST READ IN ORDER)

CHECKMATE DUET SERIES

ROOMMATE DUET SERIES

LAWTON RIDGE DUET SERIES

INTERCONNECTED STAND-ALONES

BISHOP BROTHERS SERIES

CIRCLE B RANCH SERIES

BISHOP FAMILY ORIGIN

LOVE IN ISOLATION SERIES

ONLY ONE SERIES

MAKE ME SERIES

Find the entire Kennedy Fox reading order at
Kennedyfoxbooks.com/reading-order

Printed in Great Britain
by Amazon

40470862R00138